The Midnight Man

A Novel by
Chelsea Gouin

Pages Promotions, LLC
1963 Bowers Street
Birmingham, Michigan 48009
www.PagesPromotions.com

© 2019 Chelsea Gouin
Published by Pages Promotions, LLC
www.PagesPromotions.com
All Rights Reserved

Print ISBN: 978-1628282160

E-book ISBN: 978-1628282177

Library of Congress Control Number: Pending

Dedication

This book is dedicated to Matthew Burson, because I promised him.

Bear for always being my Number One.

And to Gramcrackers, Always.

Acknowledgements

The old saying goes, "It takes a village to raise a child". And it takes twice that much to write a book! I have so many people to be thankful for or this pet project of mine would never have grown into the beast it is now.

First, to Gabriel Mero, Jessica Parrish, Ashley Frank, and Lindsay LaPonse. They were the ones who read the very first draft of this story, and despite it being a hot mess, encouraged me to make it better.

Special thanks to Shonda whose Faith inspires me each and every day.

I have to thank Ms. Gigi Lovelette; my ride or die that's always believed in me even when I don't.

Melanie, my friend and rock... she deserves so much praise for the love and support she's shown me through the years. Literally wouldn't be here without her.

To everyone at Grand Pacific House Museum in New Baltimore! Too many of you to list, but every one of you has supported me, listened to my schemes, and appointed me a Chairman of Fun. Thank you, you crazy bunch!!

My sisters who will probably never read this book because they hate books and horror... but they love me and want to see me successful. Thanks for being there, girls.

To all the Indie Authors I've met on this journey, especially Misty, Andy, Bailey, and Jordan. Thanks for welcoming me with open arms to the family and cheering me on.

Of course, to my Gramcrackers, though she is no longer with us, her spirit was with me. She always hated that I wrote horror, wanting me to write "normal" stories, but she nevertheless listened to my crazy ideas and encouraged me every step of the way.

Finally, to my amazing editor Connor and my Literary Mama Diana! You two saw something in a silly story I'd written, kicked me out of the nest and made me an author! Thank you from the bottom of my heart for believing in me and this story. Truly blessed to have worked with both of you!

Chapter One

"Before we sign off, witches, I just wanted to remind everyone this will be our last vlog for...well a while." Charlie rustled her short, dark hair awkwardly. "I'll be leaving for film school next week, and it wouldn't feel right reporting without my partner." She smiled over at Alex.

"And you know I'll just be dying without Charlie to keep me in check!" he winked into the camera lens.

With a smirk, Charlie did her signature sign off but didn't push the power button on

---

her camera. "I think I'll wait to edit this until after I'm all moved in... it'll be something to keep me busy, anyway…"

Alex regarded his best friend fondly. They'd been friends for years now, bonding over a shared love of film and the paranormal. When things got particularly rough for Charlie, their bond had transformed, and he stepped into the "protective older brother" role.

"You should have gotten this scholarship," Charlie muttered, grabbing a stuffed cat perched next to her on the bed.

Alex rolled his eyes, Charlie was going to be a great director someday; she was passionate, creative, and had a vision that Alex hadn't seen in any other movie he'd watched. He just wished she believed in herself like everyone else did. "I'm really more of a script writer and editor. It's why we make such a perfect team!"

Charlie shot him an exasperated look. "And that's why Dr. Halverson always sang your praises?"

"He obviously had the hots for me," Alex winked. "Yeah, so some community college professor enjoyed one short film of mine. You impressed an entire board and won a full ride! Own it, lady!"

Charlie methodically stroked the plush cat's fur. "It just won't be the same without you nerds! I'll be over five hours away..."

Not knowing how to cheer her up, Alex scooped up the camera and zoomed in to Charlie's morose face. "No more sadness! We're partying tonight!"

"Yeah... one last hooray before I'm off to exile..." She let out a heavy sigh before managing a small smile. "Maybe I'll be able to get some footage for my freshman project?"

"Oh, definitely!" Alex said enthusiastically, "and if that doesn't work out, I can always film your and Sydney's sex tape."

Charlie threw the stuffed cat at Alex, laughing only when it managed to bounce off his head.

Chapter Two

Charlie drummed her fingers against the steering wheel in time to the music. Alex was fiddling with the settings on the video camera, turning the knobs and making various lights flash on the control panel as he played with the zoom and contrast settings.

"So, how did Sydney take the news that you invited Nikki tonight?" Alex asked, swinging the lens on to Charlie.

"As you'd expect," Irritated, Charlie brushed back an errant wisp of her dark hair that had settled over her eye as she flicked an annoyed look at Alex. "Aren't I supposed to be the director? What good will this footage of me be, anyway?"

Alex laughed. "Lighten up! You always say you never know when a shot might come in handy, I'm just helping out!" He propped the camera on to the dashboard, refocusing, so both he and Charlie were in the shot. "Besides, Sydney's house takes forever to get to!"

Charlie chuckled. "Under twenty minutes!"

"It's basically in the middle of nowhere!" Alex smirked as he teased.

"She has some property in the woods; nice and private." Charlie smiled, letting the happy memories overtake her.

"Are you packed up?"

"Mostly, some of my film equipment needs special cases that I don't have quite yet." She paused. "I'm totally stalling. I've lived with Sydney for a year. I'm not sure I'm ready to leave her yet."

Alex fiddled with a loose thread on his fingerless gloves. He didn't do emotional conversations, and yet here he was, again. Alex always felt especially awkward when Charlie got emotional or touchy-feely; she would be completely unpredictable, and Alex worried he'd say the wrong thing. He hoped that tonight's party proved the pick-me-up Charlie needed. All her friends together for one last farewell.

Both of them were pulled out of their reveries when Alex's phone chimed an obnoxious jingle. "Nikki!" They both announced together.

"It's a text," Alex announced. *Damn*, he thought, *Charlie's bummer mood always makes me uncomfortable.* Silently he thanked Nikki's intuition to save him. "She says she's running a bit late, but she'll definitely be there tonight. With food."

Charlie smiled. "Well, that's something you can always rely on her for."

Chapter Three

"Babe! I'm home." Charlie called as she and Alex entered the house. He was still holding the camera, trained on her reactions. "What is this? A documentary on me?" She blushed when she heard the telltale whirl of the camera's zoom feature.

Sydney slid into the foyer, her face brightening as soon as she laid eyes on her girlfriend. She flung her arms around Charlie, squeezing. They'd been dating for almost two years now, and Sydney was honestly in love with Charlie. The woman understood her like no one else ever had. Sure, she was heartbroken that Charlie was leaving next week for school but understood it as a necessary evil.

Charlie swooped down and kissed Sydney, nothing more than a quick pressure of lips on lips, but to Sydney, it was everything. Her knees felt weak, and her heart fluttered as if it was their first time.

"Don't mind me," Alex joked, a grin wide over his face as he trained the camera on the couple.

Sydney blushed. "You're filming?" She straightened her blouse and righted her thin wire glasses, smiling shyly into the lens. "I didn't realize, sorry!"

Charlie wrestled the camera from Alex, swinging the focus to her partner in crime. "Yeah, I wanted to get some footage of everyone before I left. So many films can use good party scenes. Plus, it'll help when I'm feeling extra lonely."

Sydney pouted, feeling the mood switch. "Oh, well..." she looked at Alex, who was avoiding both their eyes. "I got everything set up, and Darren is here!"

"Darren?" Alex perked up. He smoothed down his black hair, doing a quick, self-conscious reflection check in the oval mirror, hanging just behind them. "Does he look hot?"

Sydney rolled her eyes. "You know he's straight, right?"

"Doesn't stop Alex," Charlie joked. "Babe, you didn't have to set anything up, I told you." She leaned in and brushed another quick kiss on her girlfriend's cheek.

Alex awkwardly cleared his throat, drawing the two away again. "Did you get James' text? About that game he found online?"

Sydney chewed on her bottom lip. "Yeah, but I didn't read too much about it."

Charlie squeezed her hand. "It's spooky, for sure. Alex and I looked it up and did some research; I think it'd be fun to try." Sydney still looked skeptical. "Or not."

"Throw your jackets and whatever in the study," she gestured to the room across from them, connected to the foyer with a dark wooden frame. "I haven't really used it much since Dad passed…"

Charlie squeezed Sydney's hand, knowing her girlfriend still suffered the ache from the loss. A loud beep interrupted their moment. "Damn, batteries are low."

Chapter Four

7:20 p.m.   Kitchen, Handheld Camera

"I think it's on... the red light is blinking. That means it's on, right?" Darren asked, surveying the screen suspiciously. He gave a cheeky grin to his own image showing on the display screen. He also saw the exasperated expressions on the rest of the crew's faces in response. Shortly after Alex and Charlie's arrival, they were joined by their other friends, Madicyn, Whitney, and James.

"Does it say record? I think it's supposed to say record somewhere on that screen." Madicyn sidled up next to him, her chest pressed against his bicep as she leaned closer. "Yeah, see where it says REC, that means it's working."

Darren tried not to openly cringe at what seemed like Madicyn's hundredth attempt to get him to pay attention to her. They had history, but he was over her shallowness. "Isn't Nikki supposed to be here?" he asked the rest of the assembled group.

"Yes, she texted me a few minutes ago. It's raining pretty hard, and she got stuck in some traffic," Whitney replied, pulling up the message on her phone.

"Isn't she supposed to be bringing the pizza? Who put her in charge of food? We all know she's usually caught up in some drama and she's never on time." James replied.

Sydney sipped her soda, choosing not to comment an "I told you so" that would only rile up Charlie, and she didn't want to fight on what was supposed to be a fun night.

"Who needs pizza?" Darren asked, his grin widening as he gestured to the counter. "We have other treats!"

He was referring to the odd collection of alcohol assembled. When Sydney said "BYOB," the group obliged. Rum, whiskey, and wine in various colored bottles clustered together, promising a good time.

"What's a margarita bucket?" Madicyn asked, tapping the plastic tub.

James grinned and cracked open the purple lid. "Everything we need for a good time! Mix and salt... for the rims." He winked at Madicyn. "Just add tequila, and we're all set!"

Sydney groaned. "Do we remember the last time this group consumed tequila?"

The friends shared a laugh. Charlie quietly observed the merriment.

It was certainly a rather motley crew she'd assembled. She took a sip from her plastic cup, observing her friends. First, there was Sydney, beautiful blonde-haired blue-eyed Sidney; Charlie was positive she was the love of her life.

Then there was Alex, her goth best friend and the closest thing she had to a brother, the only family she really had left now that her actual family disowned her.

Next to him was Madicyn, her loose black curls framed her pale face, looking only slightly put-out that she was being ignored.

Charlie met Madicyn in broadcasting class. Madicyn was a student news anchor, and Charlie was behind the camera, which led the two to work together on many creative projects.

Darren had joined the group as Madicyn's boyfriend and instantly assimilated to the mayhem that the group caused. He had rock star good looks, with sandy locks perched atop a tan face and charming smile. He was everyone's favorite playboy, and he knew it.

Charlie had known James, and his twin sister Whitney, literally her entire life, and couldn't imagine life without either of their night and day personalities. The Rushing twins were similar in appearance, each having skin the color of cafe au lait and eyes of melted chocolate, accentuated by thick lashes. But beyond looks, they were different in every sense. James liked being the center of attention and found humor in every situation. Whitney preferred to stick to the shadows and quietly enjoy the company.

With Whitney came her best friend, the perky blonde Nikki, a neighbor and friend of Alex's and, also, the wedge between the group. Nikki had a tendency to be outspoken and liked to be in everyone's business; Charlie felt like it was coming from a good place but knew Nikki's opinions and help weren't always welcome. Nikki helped Alex have the courage to come out about his sexuality and embrace it. However, when Sydney broke up with Charlie early on, an impossible rift formed between the two. Even after Sydney and Charlie patched things up, neither Nikki nor Sydney were willing to take back the hateful things that had been said between them.

"Babe," Sydney whispered, lightly touching Charlie's arm to drag her from her thoughts. Talk around the table had turned to recent movies, the stress of the upcoming fall semester, and the frequent storms that plagued them lately. Sydney was watching Charlie though, concern etched into her features. "You okay?"

Charlie smiled, leaning her head on top of Sydney's. "With you? Always." She muttered, taking in her friends around the table. Sometimes she felt like she was two different people, the only glue holding the group together, but she was glad to see them setting aside their differences for tonight. The laughter had grown to a point where they almost missed the knock at the door.

Charlie scooped up the camera and followed Alex to the door. It swung open to reveal Nikki, her rain jacket dripping onto the welcome mat. Nonetheless, she grinned and held up two armfuls of cardboard boxes and plastic bags.

"Party's here!" Nikki proclaimed, kicking off her soaked tennis shoes. "What's with the camera? Can't stop working for one second, Ms. Director?"

Balancing the camera on top of her shoulder, Charlie leaned in for an awkward one-armed hug. "I have that huge film project by the end of the semester, figured we were entertaining enough."

Sydney stood off to the side, mouth tucked in a thin disproving line. Her arms remained firmly crossed, and she offered no greeting or assistance; Nikki returned the sentiments, choosing instead to tease Alex about his new haircut as they walked to the kitchen.

Chapter Five

7:40 p.m. Kitchen, Handheld Camera

"Hey! Be careful with that!" Alex called from across the kitchen. He watched helplessly as Nikki spun around the table, shoving the lens in everyone's face screaming "cheese" at each one.

"Lighten up, Alex!" She giggled and turned the camera on James. "Okay, James, say something interesting... anything!"

"Darling, you couldn't afford the fees for my appearance." He cocked an eyebrow and sipped from his solo cup.

"Ugh, riveting as always." Nikki rolled her eyes, shifting the focus to Whitney.

"What's up, Whit?"

Whitney fiddled with her thick braid, a light blush creeping up her face, highlighting her feminine features. "Um, I'm not sure what... to say…"

Nikki pouted. "Geez, tough crowd. How about you, Darren? Anything you'd like to say?" As she panned over to the other side of the table, she noticed Madicyn's sour expression. Like it was Nikki's fault that Darren was adorable... and single.

James also noticed Madicyn pouting and snaked his arm around her shoulders. "Lighten up, sour puss! It's a party!"

Madicyn attempted to shrug him off. "It was a bit livelier half an hour ago," she muttered.

"Why are you acting like this?" James wasn't intimidated by her glare. "Bitchy-ex doesn't suit you. You're better than this."

Darren grinned and winked. "I'm ready to really start this party." He shuffled through his duffle bag, which he'd conveniently stashed under his feet. He fished out a paper bag and paused, making sure the entirety of the party was watching, before brandishing a bottle of Fireball.

"Surprise!"

Nikki squealed. "Perfect! Who wants a shot!"

Sydney scoffed, remembering how sloppy Nikki got after a few shots. But the cinnamon whiskey was a staple. The first booze Darren had smuggled into a cast party when they'd only been sixteen; it would be good for nostalgia, especially if a certain blonde abstained. She snuck a glance at Charlie, who was now looking on in amusement. What did Charlie see in Nikki, honestly?

Madicyn plucked the bottle from Darren's grip. "I'll go first!" She took a swig of the whiskey before passing it on, away from Nikki.

Whatever, Nikki smirked, *I don't need liquid courage to ask Darren out tonight.* Clearly, it wouldn't take much of an effort if his stolen glances were any indication. Her thoughts were interrupted from a sputtering to her right. She spun the camera on to Alex as he choked.

"Shit!" He gasped, trying to swallow gulps of water. "I think that's it for me. You're up, Nikki."

Chapter Six

8:30 p.m.   Handheld Camera

"Alex is going to be soooo mad at you, Nikki!" Whitney giggled breathlessly as she darted up the stairs behind her best friend. "Stealing his camera! You know it's practically his lifeline lately!"

Nikki pulled Whitney into the bathroom at the top of the stairs, locking the door behind her. She spun the camera, so the lens was focusing on her flushed face. "Alex! When you are inevitably watching all this later, I hope you will forgive me. However, this thing is practically glued to your hands all the time. Your turn to live a little on the other side of the camera." She rolled her eyes and jammed a few buttons on the side.

"What are you doing?" Whitney giggled again. "The buttons are labeled, you know!"

"And if I hadn't done so many shots already, I'd probably be able to read all this fine print!" Nikki growled. She hit a few more buttons experimentally before carelessly setting the camera on the counter and plopping onto the toilet lid, letting Whitney have full access to the mirror over the sink. Pulling out her compact to check her smoky eyeliner, she eyed the sparsely decorated, cramped room. "You know, since Charlie moved in with Sydney, she's never invited me over."

Whitney side-eyed her friend as she dug in her clutch for her lipstick. "I mean, can you blame her? You and Sydney have had bad blood for quite some time now."

Nikki rolled her eyes again, running her hand through her blonde locks. "Can you blame me? The way she treated Charlie was unforgivable!"

"Charlie seems to have gotten over it," Whitney hummed as she swiped on a layer of lipstick. The peach shade looked even brighter against her dark skin.

"Well, maybe we can reconcile over Christmas Break." Nikki shrugged dismissively, ready to discuss anything but Sydney. "I've got other people to win over tonight."

Whitney moved to lean against the wall, crossing her arms over her chest as she watched Nikki admire her own reflection in the mirror. "Yeah, I noticed you and Darren checking each other out."

Nikki's face brightened as a grin stretched over her face. "He was checking me out too?" She squealed. "I knew he would wise up once Madicyn dumped him... again." She scooped up a handful of her hair and began twisting it into a ponytail atop her head.

"Nik," Whitney tried to use as reproachful a tone as she could. "Darren is a nice guy, and I know how long you've been crushing on him... but this is supposed to be about Charlie tonight. Maybe hold off on the seducing until a more appropriate time?"

Nikki brushed the comment off with a noncommittal shrug, applying another layer of her favorite strawberry lip gloss and admiring her reflection.

"I actually wanted to talk to you about this for a while, and I know a party is probably the wrong time to do this, but I'm your friend, and I wanted you to hear it from me." Whitney picked at her nail polish. She knew this was going to be awkward, but she felt like someone had to talk to Nikki about her attitude. "It's just that you're a great friend Nikki, no one doubts that... just sometimes you get so wrapped up in drama, stuff that's not really even your business... and you have a tendency to make it about you..."

Nikki spun around, her ponytail almost whipping Whitney's nose. "Are you calling me self-centered?"

"No! No, I just meant..." Whitney watched Nikki's blue eyes narrow as she processed the information. Definitely not the right moment for a heart to heart. "Just try and remember we're celebrating Charlie tonight, kay?"

"But you'll help me with Darren, right?" Nikki smirked.

"Of course." Whitney shrugged weakly. "Let's not forget to return Alex's camera either, or we'll be the stars of his next movie... about murder!"

Nikki giggled. "You're such a great friend Whitney!"

Chapter Seven

9:30 p.m. Handheld Camera

"Okay, Charlie," Alex said to the camera. "I don't know when you'll see this, but I know when you do, it'll be because you're feeling extra lonely."

Alex broke off from the party under the pretense of having to make a phone call, ducking into the abandoned study. He didn't think the group particularly cared as they were pretty wrapped up in a heated debate over who had the funniest card in the round of Cards Against Humanity.

"Charlie, Charlie," Alex sighed, sweeping his bangs from his hazel eyes. "You know I'm going to miss you, but I know this will only launch your career as the best director ever! And don't forget to hire me as your editor!" He paused as memories wrapped around him. "Remember our first movie we... well... attempted to make?" He chuckled. "The stains on the carpet never did come out! Well, listen, I am already stewing on an idea for another project, one we can maybe do when you come back for Christmas break ..."

Alex broke off when he heard stumbling and tipsy giggles behind him. Crouching further into the shadow of the hallway, he peered around the corner to spy Madicyn and Sydney with their arms around each other in the living room.

"Oh, Syd!" Madicyn giggled, pushing her raven black hair back into its perfect place. She patted her friend on the shoulder and flopped onto the leather couch. "This was a great idea... all of it."

Sydney perched next to Madicyn, her lips settling on a soft smile. "Charlie deserves a nice send-off."

Madicyn smirked over the rim of her Solo cup. "And Nikki deserves what's coming to her too." With a large gulp, Madicyn let the fire of the alcohol consume her and burn all the insecurities a certain blonde seemed to always agitate. "Can you believe how obvious she's being with Darren?"

"Yeah, but I also noticed James sneaking glances your way too," Sydney smirked.

"Well," Madicyn laughed. "I do miss his dreadlocks, but that shaved head of his is still looking pretty fine."

Both girls giggled when the said shaved head popped into the room to ask if they wanted to sit the next round out or if they'd be joining back into the game.

"Shucksyputz!" Sydney exclaimed as some of her beverage sloshed over the rim of her plastic cup.

"Oh no!" Madicyn giggled. "You don't still use fake swear words, do you?"

Sydney's face turned a glowing red. "Well, with Daddy being a preacher, he didn't allow dirty words under his roof... so the made-up ones became more of a habit."

"Well... sugar honey iced tea! Let's go kick some butt at this card game!" Madicyn teased.

Alone once again, Alex spun the camera to himself. "Well, Charlie... we certainly are a versatile bunch. If it wasn't for you always rallying our little motley crew, I don't know if we'd have all lasted this long. So, enjoy your time away from us little people, I can't wait to make another movie with you!" He blew a kiss before ending the recording.

Chapter Eight

10:00 p.m. Handheld Camera

"I really hope this is working…" James mumbled, spinning some knobs as he tried to get the lens to focus on his face.

Satisfied his face appeared clear on the screen; he cleared his throat. "Boy, is this awkward. As you can see, I managed to finally pry this thing out of Alex's fingers because, damn, you'd think this was an extra appendage or something." James huffed softly.

While Alex had been a little reluctant to hand his camera over to James, he knew he'd just have to trust him this time. James was known to be a little more of a prankster than most. But this was part of some sappy idea Alex had so, he let James run off with his precious camera, the thing looking child-sized in James' massive hands.

Now alone, James was struggling to come up with what to say. Emotions weren't his forte, he used humor to deflect anything deep or meaningful. But Charlie was practically a second sister after living next to each other for so long, and he was going to miss her.

"Well, Charlie, I guess it goes without saying that I'll miss you. You're about the only one that understands my sarcasm." He gave a quick smirk. "And give it back. Remember when I forgot my lines during rehearsal? You were directing that play and were just so worried about it being perfect... it was dress rehearsal, not even show night, and I thought you were going to kill me right there on stage for freezing up." James sighed. "Yeah, it won't be the same without you, Charlie. But you're going to be amazing, I just know it!"

"You too?"

James glanced up to see Whitney leaning on the doorframe. Her dark eyebrow rose, and her mouth tightened in contemplation. "I thought Alex was going to have a heart attack when Nikki stole his camera, now you've snuck off with it?"

He merely waved the camera carelessly. "This was Alex's idea; you think I'd have gotten away with his precious camera if he hadn't thought of it? He wants everyone to record a send-off for Charlie, but she can't know about it. Unfortunately, there's no smooth way to do this."

Whitney kept her eyes narrowed, searching her brother's face for any hint of a lie. As twins, the pair was used to the tired questions of how in sync they were. James was always the center of attention, the life of the party, but his sister was the wallflower, happier to observe than orchestrate.

"I'm surprised you found me," James said as he spun the camera to focus on Whitney. "I specifically chose the study because no one uses it. Plus, you're usually always attached to someone's side."

Whitney scoffed. "What's that supposed to mean?"

James shrugged. "I don't know, Whit. It's just every time we go out, you seem to pick a friend to stick to for the night."

"Yeah, that's me. James's sister, Nikki's friend," Whitney rolled her eyes. "How about we try just Whitney Rushing? I'm my own freaking person."

"All right! I get it!" He laughed. "My little sister wants to be recognized."

"You're only older by *three minutes*!"

"There you two are!" Charlie bounded over to them, pushing a Solo cup into James' hand. "And there's Alex's camera. I thought he looked different." They all shared a chuckle. "He's going on about some new script he's working on, pretty sure he's planning on casting you two."

"What's it about this time? Zombies?" Whitney asked, brushing aside a loose wisp of hair.

Charlie sipped her own drink. "Nah, something about a friend accidentally getting possessed after using an old Ouija board."

Whitney shivered. "What a thought! I would never touch one of those!"

"Didn't you say you don't believe in that sort of stuff?" James asked, taking a giant gulp from the cup. "I believe it was the last haunted house script Alex wrote you were so adamant against."

"It's not that I don't believe, it's I don't want to tempt anything that may be there." she corrected.

Charlie laughed. "Well, let's just be grateful Alex didn't bring an actual Ouija board."

Chapter Nine

11:00 p.m Living Room, Handheld Camera

It was getting late, and Charlie could see, from her spot on the couch, the guests losing interest. Whitney, perched on the far end of the couch, was already talking about heading home to finish up some project for work, trying to pull Nikki's attention from Darren. James was lounging on one of the twin overstuffed armchairs across the room, glued to his phone; Darren and Alex were impatiently fiddling with the radio situated in the large entertainment center taking up the leftmost wall. Madicyn, was wedged between the two, to try and remain relevant. Sydney seemed content, curled up against Charlie, sipping on a glass of wine and occasionally whispering "remember when's."

"Hey Charlie, Syd," James called from his spot across the living room. "Do you happen to have a candle supply?"

Charlie zoomed in to focus on James. "Like birthday candles?"

He smirked. "No, full-size candles, think decorative. Enough for everyone here."

Sydney straightened up, a bit anxious with the questioning. "Sure. We have some of Dad's old church candles in the basement, I'm sure of it. Why?"

"I think I've found the perfect party game, the one I texted you about? It's called the Midnight Game."

Nikki snorted. "The Midnight Game? What the hell does that even mean?"

James held up his phone. "It's not a joke, Nikki. From the sounds of it, things can get... deadly."

"Now you've got my interest," Darren grinned. Scary games were the perfect opportunity to get close with people, and Nikki didn't look like the brave sort. He crossed away from the radio under the pretense of reading over James' shoulder when, in reality, it was to detach Madicyn from his arm.

"I don't know," Sydney bit her lip and looked nervously over at Charlie.

Madicyn rolled her eyes. "What is it? Some kind of Bloody Mary game? We're not twelve, James."

"Yeah, the concept is the same anyway. You summon the Midnight Man at midnight, and have to survive until 3:33 a.m. The website warns it's not for the faint of heart."

Whitney twirled her braid, her gaze hardening on her brother. "Did you say summon? That sounds like a little more than your average party game. What exactly is this 'Midnight Man'?"

James let his eyes scroll through the text on his screen a moment before shrugging. "I mean, it doesn't say, so I'm assuming some sort of spirit?"

"Sounds more like a demon," Nikki shivered. "What do you think, Alex? The paranormal realm is more your thing."

"I'm no expert!" Alex chuckled. "But from the research I have done on the topic, a demon takes a bit more effort to summon than a few candles." He glanced at Charlie. "Where's your tablet? I'll pull the rules up for everyone to look at."

Charlie dug in the drawer of the side table. She always kept her tablet close to the couch. "James texted us about this game earlier," she explained as she handed the tablet to Alex. "We thought it might be fun."

Alex quickly pulled up a webpage and passed the tablet around, displaying the rules for the game.

Chapter Ten

The Midnight Game

The Midnight Game is a pagan ritual used to punish those who've broken pagan Law. There is a chance of danger or death for those who choose to play "the Midnight Game." It is highly recommended that you do not play the Midnight Game! But for those seeking a thrill or willing to tempt the occult, there are a few simple rules...

Instructions

The game must begin at exactly 12:00 A.M. the required materials include paper, a drop of the players' blood, candles, lighters, and salt for each player.

Step 1: Write your full name on a piece of paper and add one drop of your own blood.

Step 2: Turn off all the lights. At your front door, place your piece of paper. Light your candle and place it on top of the paper.

Step 3: Knock on the door twenty-two times with the final knock ending at exactly midnight. Open the door, blow out your candle, and close the door. You've now allowed the Midnight Man into your home.

Step 4: Immediately relight your candle.

The game has started. You have until 3:33 A.M to avoid the Midnight Man. You must move around with your candle to prevent him from finding you. If your candle goes out, the Midnight Man is near you, and you must relight it within ten seconds. If you are unsuccessful, surround yourself with a circle of salt for protection. You must remain in the circle until the end of the game. Failure of both of these steps will result in being a victim to the Midnight Man. He will leave your home at 3:33 A.M.

Addition: Indications the Midnight Man near includes a drop in temperature, a black figure moving in the shadows, and soft whispering. It's advised you move from the area to avoid him.

IMPORTANT!

Do Not turn on any lights!

Do Not use a flashlight or phone!

Do Not go to sleep!

Do Not use a lighter in lieu of a candle.

And definitely, DO NOT attempt to provoke the Midnight Man!

Alex looked around the group eagerly, trying to gauge everyone's reactions. "Well, what do you think? It may give you an opportunity for some footage... for your project, Charlie. It could be like the movie, *Blair Witch*. We could post it on the vlog, it'd be like our very own *Myth Busters*!"

Charlie laughed, "Well..."

"C'mon..." James chided, his eyes sparkling with secret mischief. "These are some pretty basic rules... no sleeping, can only use candles as light, can't stay in the same room... and don't let the Midnight Man catch you." He paused, eyes scanning the tablet screen. "Or else! Apparently, this game could end in torture or death if the rules are broken." He chuckled.

Alex nodded eagerly. "This post was an old one from Reddit, but there's similar stories on Creepy Pasta, YouTube, and a ton of other horror blogs! People say it can get really scary!"

"This sounds pretty serious," Whitney muttered, toying with her braid again.

Nikki shivered. "Yeah, I'm not feeling this one. Talks of torture and death... not to mention using your own blood!"

"We've done stuff like this before, Sydney offered, tapping her glass anxiously. "I mean, none of them required blood, but..."

Alex tucked the tablet back into the drawer. "Really? I thought you all would be as excited as I was. This is probably some ghost story to make an Internet meme, but it could be the real deal."

"Yeah, little girls," James grinned, cracking his knuckles. "Leave the spooky stuff to us!"

Darren brushed back his hair, giving one of his most winning smiles. "Count me in!"

"Well, this is Charlie's party..." Nikki slid her gaze over to her friend.

Charlie glanced at Sydney. Her knuckles were white as they grasped her wine glass tighter. Nikki and Whitney were both watching her with wide, uncertain eyes. *Guess it's my choice.* "Why the hell not? It might be fun."

James and Darren high-fived, and Alex sent Charlie a satisfied nod. "Is your extra equipment still upstairs? Everyone can help with set up."

"Yeah, some of my old cameras are upstairs in the spare bedroom. Guess it's a good thing I haven't finished packing!"

"What about candles?" Whitney asked. "You sure we'll have enough?"

Sydney paused, calculating silently. "I think so... I haven't gone through all the boxes. We have a couple decorative votives from Christmas for sure."

"And salt? The rules said everyone should have salt on them." Nikki asked.

Sydney glanced at Charlie for assurance. "I know we have a thing of Morton in the cupboard..."

"James' margarita bucket has salt!" Madicyn offered.

Darren rubbed his hands together eagerly. "Sounds like we have everything! Let's do this!"

"Wait!" Sydney called as everyone began to shuffle out. "Let's not use the study; everyone's things are in there. And absolutely no one in the Master Bedroom!" She gestured down the hall, opposite of the kitchen. "Upstairs should be okay. Straight up the stairs in the linen closet, immediately to the left is my bedroom, and in the middle of the hallway is a bathroom. The other end of the hallway is Charlie's old bedroom, but it's so full of boxes she's been packing, it might be hard to navigate."

Alex quickly scribbled a layout on a spare napkin. "I put x's where the cameras should get the best angles. I figure the basement is empty enough; you don't need a drawing of that!" He waved to the far corner of the living room. "If we set one there, it should cover the majority of the room and just the archway to the kitchen."

The group dispersed, leaving behind Sydney and Charlie to a now quiet living room. Sidney tucked a strand of her long hair behind her ear, shifting nervously. "Are you sure about this, babe?"

The couple jumped apart upon a loud thud to their left. James was grinning, with a white bucket at his feet. "Hope I'm not interrupting anything." He winked.

"Is that road salt?" Sydney asked.

James shrugged. "Figured bigger the salt, the better the protection. I saw this out in the garage when we first got here." He pointed his thumb over his shoulder.

Charlie chuckled. "Whatever makes you feel safe. Just be sure to divvy the salt evenly for everyone." Once he left, Charlie shrugged. "This is all in good fun, right? Come on, we better help them set up the cameras around the house."

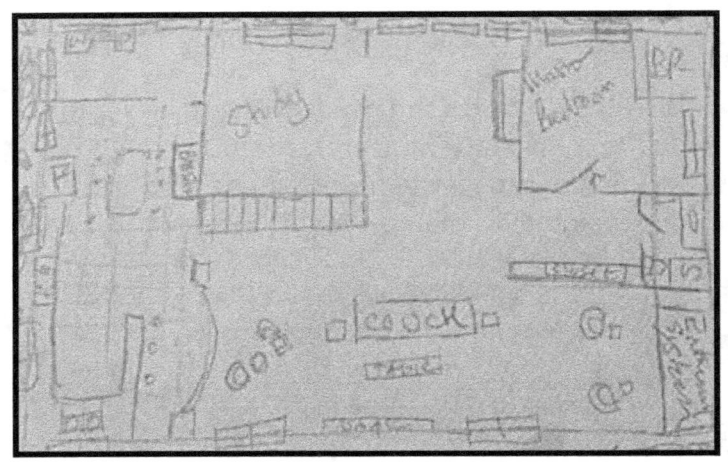

up stairs

Chapter Eleven

11:07 p.m.   Basement Camera

Madicyn gently placed the camera on top of the tripod. "What do you think, Whitney? In this corner or maybe more to the right?"

Whitney tilted the camera just slightly to the right. "There! Now the view covers the stairs too." She glanced at the display. The angle presented a wide shot of the unfinished basement, of the bare concrete floors and plain stucco walls, the dark corners, the home of spiders scuttling about, and other creepy crawlies. The only thing breaking up the sparse basement was the metal shelving units shoved in the corner, the shelves straining from their heavy burdens.

Madicyn pawed through the boxes of dusty knick-knacks and religious memorabilia. She shifted a heavy tote filled with crucifixes to the other side. "Sydney really needs to label all these!"

Whitney giggled, moving an ornate mirror to rest on the adjacent unit. "Some of this was her mom's. I know Charlie said Sydney hardly mentions her, but I remember how hard she took it when her dad passed."

"Found them!" Madicyn exclaimed, pulling out various sized candles. Some were squat and white, others taller and brightly colored, and finally a twin set of red housed in glass tubes.

"I guess we're all set down here, then!" Whitney said as she helped gather the candles. "Oops, we almost forgot to put on the night vision mode! Otherwise, we'd just be recording darkness!"

"I mean, what else are we recording?" Madicyn rolled her eyes and checked the hook-up a second time. She disdainfully surveyed the bare walls, looking particularly drab alongside the unfinished concrete floor. "Do we honestly believe this 'Midnight Man' is real?"

Whitney shrugged. "I try to keep an open mind about these things."

Chapter Twelve

11:10 p.m. Bathroom Camera

"Really, James? The bathroom?" Alex laughed, watching as his friend adjusted the angle to point out the door. The camera was wedged between the claw-footed tub and the wall, the bathroom being small enough that the majority would fit in the frame.

"Hey, you wanted a secret space for people to record a sendoff for Charlie; what better place than the obscure, upstairs bathroom? I don't know about you, but I use the bathroom pretty frequently, perfect excuse to sneak off." He smirked. "Besides, if someone needs privacy, they can always close the curtain." He demonstrated by

Chelsea Gouin   55   The Midnight Man sliding the curtain around the tub, blocking the camera's view of the bubblegum pink walls and pearly white tiles.

Chapter Thirteen

11:10 p.m. Kitchen Camera

"Like this?" Nikki called over her shoulder.

Charlie chuckled. The display showed a generous view down Nikki's shirt. "Try tilting it up a bit more," she suggested. Once Nikki fixed the angle, Charlie tightened the bolts on the stand perched on the back-kitchen counter. "And now we have a great wide view of the kitchen." She double-checked, making sure the camera was tilted just so, in order to see beyond the L-shaped counter and to the adjacent basement door. "I already have one up on a tripod in the living room, which will just cover the archway and the kitchen table. And Syd is getting a camera set up upstairs. I think we're set."

"You're not at all nervous about this?" Nikki asked, twirling a lock of her blonde hair that had fallen out of its ponytail. "I mean, I'm sure it's just some stupid urban legend... but..." she shifted her weight a moment before spitting out the last bit. "What if it's not?" She let out a heavy sigh. "I'm doing this for you, Charlie. You know I'll always be there for you."

"Don't worry Nikki, I promise not to let the Boogey Man get you."

Chapter Fourteen

11:15 p.m.   Bedroom Camera

"That should do it!" Sydney stepped to the front of the camera after re-adjusting the wiring. The camera was in her bedroom, tucked in the back corner next to her bed, pointing out into the upstairs hallway. She was lucky to have room, what with the stacks of suitcases and moving boxes shoved in every available space, posters of favorite films and Broadway playbills tacked on her mint green walls just peeking out from the chaos. The camera caught enough of the cramped room, including part of her vanity mirror. Right now, Darren was reflected on the display, but his focus was outside of the room. "Penny for your thoughts, D?"

Darren rustled his hair and let out a heavy sigh. "Can I ask what happened between you and Nikki?"

Sydney paused in her adjustments, considering the unexpected question. "Well…" she fumbled some more with the buttons, pretending to focus the lens. "I forgot you were on the football team and didn't really join our little group until after all this went down. It wasn't easy for me to admit I had feelings for Charlie. I mean, Alex was just so comfortable being gay, and Charlie seemed to embrace that side of her too… I thought maybe me liking her was just a phase because I was so uncomfortable." She glanced quickly at Darren and found she had his full attention. "Try to understand… I was just part of so many clubs! Mom left us right before I started freshman year, so I threw myself into different after-school groups. I was in student newspaper, yearbook, the dance team, tech crew for drama to paint the sets…"

Darren gestured to the bed, his eyes still kind. She flopped carelessly beside him. "So, you were busy?"

"Yes," Sydney's eyes glazed over. "I was wearing myself thin. Charlie was stage manager and ran the cameras for broadcasting class. She was always so put together, and charming..." a small smile lifted the corners of her lips. "I fell for her quickly... before I even knew it! The second her lips touched mine, my whole world changed."

Darren gave her a lopsided grin. "Oh, I know what that's like!"

"I was the one who outed her." Sydney's cheeks flushed pink with shame. "I was so confused! I never thought I was gay... and here I was kissing a girl! I told some girls on the Dance Team," she rolled her eyes. "Here I thought I was fitting in... little did I know they'd use that information to torture Charlie."

"I remember that," Darren muttered. "We had to have an assembly on cyber-bullying."

"Charlie's parents saw the posts... the ones using homophobic slurs, the crude drawings shared on Facebook," Sydney picked at the loose threads on her blouse. "Unfortunately, they weren't accepting of Charlie's lifestyle and kicked her out." She continued to pluck at her sleeve, avoiding Darren's gaze. "She asked if she could stay with me, but..."

Darren reached out to pat Sydney's shoulder, but she pulled away and began pacing, twirling her hair in agitation.

"It was all too much, too new! I was still coming to terms with my feelings, not to mention how I was going to tell Daddy! How would that have looked? The preacher's daughter, a lesbian?"

Darren smirked. "But he was cool with it when you did talk to him. Which is how Charlie eventually came to live with you."

Sydney sank back onto the bed. "Yes... he made a stupid joke about its okay because I'm a girl, but if I was a boy..." she chuckled. "Charlie was lucky to have Alex and his family willing to take her in."

Sydney shrugged, scraping off her nail polish and fidgeting.

"So you had a fight... it happens. You two just never reconciled?" Darren asked, his dark eyes inquisitive.

"It was worse than a fight," Sydney admitted. "There were texts, rumors, just real ugly stuff. We both took it way out of proportion. Long story short, I couldn't deny my true feelings for Charlie. We made up, she moved in, and we've been happy ever since. However, Nikki and I can't get past our fight."

Darren raised his manicured eyebrow. "So, it got ugly?"

"Way ugly," Sydney winced. "At one point, there was pushing and hair-pulling and a lot of screaming... from both of us." She sighed, shaking her blonde hair over her shoulders. "Anyway, Charlie assured me Nikki is well-intentioned but, really?"

Darren hugged Sydney. "Aw, Syd."

She pushed him off with a laugh. "Thanks for listening, D. I see the way you've been watching her tonight. Be careful, kay? Don't get on her bad side."

Chapter Fifteen

11:30 p.m.   Kitchen, Handheld Camera

"Blood!" Madicyn shrieked. "Wait a minute, no one said I had to be the first one to shed my blood."

James rolled his eyes, still holding the needle out to her. "Come on, Mads, suck it up. It's just a tiny pinprick. Sign your name on the paper and seal it with a drop of blood. It's the first step to the ritual."

Alex shuddered, turning the handheld camera onto Madicyn's pale face. Holding the camera also let him avoid the inevitable poke. Surveying the rest of the kitchen, he saw Charlie fold up her paper and wiggle it at him triumphantly.

"Be careful," Nikki warned Darren as he hovered a sewing needle over her offered finger. She winced at the contact but quickly smeared it on the paper without a second thought.

Now that she had completed her first step, Nikki took a generous gulp of liquor, seeing to steel herself for what was to come. With grim determination, she marched toward Sydney, who was doodling small hearts next to her name. "Can I speak to you?" Nikki asked, jerking her head toward the open archway attaching the kitchen to the living room.

"What's up, Nikki?" Sydney asked quietly, once they had broken off from the group.

Alex leaned against the kitchen table with the pretense of adjusting his camera, all the while ensuring his lens was trained on the pair.

Nikki took a deep breath, twirling an errant lock of hair that had flopped into her eye. "I know we've had our differences in the past..."

"And present..." Sydney mumbled.

Nikki's smile froze, and she took a moment to collect herself. "Very well. We've never really seen eye to eye. And as Charlie's friends, I think it's stupid and petty the way we've been acting. For Charlie's sake, can we call a truce?"

Sydney blinked a few times, her mouth opening and closing but no words coming out. "Wait, what?"

"For Charlie." Nikki shrugged. "Let's put the stupid stuff behind us and get along for her sake, it'd make her happier, and that's what's important, right?"

"Now, what have we here?" Madicyn sidled up alongside Sydney. She had dashed down the hall to the bathroom, cleaning any remaining blood from her hand. "Not the pair I'd expect to be having a tête à tête."

As if a puppet master had tightened her strings, Sydney's slouch straightened, she threw her shoulders back, and her chin pointed slightly higher in a confident stance. The warmness from her eyes seeped out to mirror the cold indifference of Madicyn's stare. "Nikki had something to say."

"That so?" Madicyn arched a dark eyebrow and settled herself against the wall, crossing her arms firmly over her chest. "Let's hear it, Nik."

Nikki's demeanor had turned decidedly frostier as well, but with a narrowed gaze, she bit out, "I was just saying this feud has lasted long enough. We're not teenagers anymore, let's grow up and move on."

Madicyn smirked. "What? I don't speak snake."

Nikki's fists clenched at her side. "This is what I'm talking about!" She cleared her throat as she noticed her friends in the next room start to glance her way. Lowering her voice, she continued, "Listen, we'll never be best friends, I'm not asking for that. I'm just trying to think of Charlie. It's important to her that we get along, so for her sake, let's do this."

"That's so like you, Nikki," Sydney also crossed her arms. "You think you're so loyal that you have everyone's back. But who do you think you're fooling?"

Madicyn leaned forward, a malicious glint in her eye. "You can have Darren. It's part of his game; he loves a good chase, and once he catches it, on to the next." She glanced into the kitchen, watching as the remaining friends giggled and taunted each other over needles and blood. "Is that part of your plan to patch things up with Charlie? Hook up with Darren at her going away party? Classy." She strutted away.

"Sydney," Nikki looked at Sydney with a desperate expression. "Please, for Charlie?"

Sydney rolled her eyes. "Do whatever, Nikki." And she too stomped away.

Nikki took a deep breath, muttering angrily to herself. "I need a drink," she said aloud after a moment and started toward the counter. That is, until she glanced at Alex. "Wait a minute, don't think you're skipping this step!"

"Shit."

Chapter Sixteen

11:55 p.m.   Handheld Camera

Charlie zoomed in on the circle of papers, focusing on each individual name assembled by the front door. At the head of the group, James was reiterating the rules.

"If your candle goes out and you're unable to light it, immediately make a circle of salt around yourself, it's the only way to protect yourself. I think we were able to put enough into each of your individual baggies to fully encircle yourselves. Do not leave the circle." He used a lighter to light Madicyn's candle, illuminating her pissed off face.

"Okay, so we wander around in the dark until... when? When does this stupid game end?"

"It's over at 3:33 a.m." Darren answered, leaning over and using his candle to light Nikki's. "We've already turned all the lights off, now we just wait until it's time to begin the summoning." He glanced at his watch. "Three minutes until midnight."

Whitney softly punched her brother's arm, "Don't forget the most important rule of all, James. Never provoke the Midnight Man!"

James offered her a cheeky grin. "Would I do that?"

"Yes!" the crowd answered in unison.

"Let me take the camera," Alex offered. "You live here, you should do the honors of knocking."

"Great," Charlie laughed as she handed it over. "Let it be my responsibility to invite the Midnight Man here."

Sydney rested her hand on Charlie's, her tense expression looking especially grim in the candle's eerie glow. Despite the group's joking, there was a tension hanging in the air. The assurances of it being a harmless game weren't placating the nerves of 'maybe it's not.' Sydney hoped this experiment was worth it and that Charlie got whatever sort of footage she was looking for.

"It's 11:59," James announced. "Remember that the twenty-second knock needs to end at midnight."

"Yeah, yeah... then we blow out our candle only to relight it," Madicyn interrupted. She glanced around with a stone-faced expression. She seemed to be the only one not getting into the spirit of the game; the fact that Nikki was holding Darren's hand wasn't helping her mood either.

Charlie began knocking as loud as she could, drowning out Alex's reminder for everyone to check their pockets for their bags of salt. Just as she hit twenty, Alex also mumbled a warning against using phones as well. "Twenty-two!" she announced just as Darren's watched beeped, indicating it was midnight.

The group collectively blew out their candles, and Charlie opened the door for a moment, greeted by a chilly gust of wind and a glimpse at the relentless rain still pouring outside. She shut the door, and those with lighters frantically flicked the small wheels to relight their candles. James used his own candle to light the votive's twin before handing it off. Others waited anxiously for a friend to use their lit wicks to ignite theirs.

"Well, we invited the Midnight Man into the house... now what?" Madicyn asked.

"Now, we play the game," Charlie answered grimly.

Chapter Seventeen

12:05 a.m. Kitchen Camera

"I'm not going to the basement," Nikki proclaimed with a shiver. "I've seen enough horror movies to know only bad things happen down there."

"Don't be such a baby," James teased, pushing past her to the basement door. "I'll go check out the basement." With that, he descended, leaving the rest of the group shifting awkwardly around the kitchen.

Charlie fiddled with her handheld camera, "Well, it won't do us any good just standing here, we're just sitting ducks. To play the game correctly, we should split up. Just remember, no leaving the house!"

Sydney grasped her girlfriend's hand immediately. "We'll go upstairs!"

"I guess I'll go make sure James doesn't do something stupid... like fall asleep." Madicyn declared with a roll of her eyes.

"I'll wait here," Whitney offered, "In case my brother does do something stupid and needs to be put back in check."

"Nikki and I will wander that way," Darren gestured toward the living room.

The group separated, leaving Alex and Whitney alone in the kitchen. She giggled nervously. "I guess I hadn't thought of what we'd do once the game started, you know?"

"Yeah," Alex grinned. "It sounded spooky when James was talking about it, but honestly... we just wander around for three and a half hours?"

Whitney pursed her lips, contemplating how much to open up to Alex. "I can't shake what James said, though... you know, if we're caught?" She let out a shaky breath.

"We'll hallucinate our deepest fears? You don't actually believe any of this, Whit, do you? It's a silly party game. Didn't you ever play *Bloody Mary*? Or try to ask questions to a Ouija board? It's the same thing. Just good, spooky fun." Alex drummed his fingers against the counter, staring at Whitney's far-off look, only half lit up by the flame of her candle.

"I guess..." she sighed. "Are you saying you don't believe anything bad will happen to us?"

Alex gave a half-hearted shrug. "I'm saying this is stuff I've read on horror blogs and YouTube comments. This is definitely a wait and see."

Whitney still didn't look convinced. "I hope there's not much to see..."

Chapter Eighteen

12:07 a.m. Living Room Camera

"Might as well get comfy," Darren said, sinking into the couch. He set his candle on the side table and stretched out with a groan. "No sleeping," he mumbled.

Nikki slowly perched on the cushion next to him, her heart rate began to pick up. Darren was just so cute, and he'd definitely shown an interest in her tonight. And now they were alone, in the dark. *Yeah, with a demon supposedly lurking around, not the time to make out Nik!* She scolded herself.

She jumped when Darren's arm slid over her shoulders, pulling her closer to his chest. "Don't be scared," he whispered in her ear. "We finally have time to get to know each other a bit better."

Chapter Nineteen

12:07 a.m. Basement Camera

"Where the hell did you sneak off to, James?" Madicyn called, squinting in the darkness. Her candle's small flame offered hardly any light, making her already poor eyesight worse.

"Behind you!" James called in her ear, letting out a whooping laugh as she jumped in the air. "Dammit, Mads! I thought you didn't believe in this crap!"

She clutched her chest as if she could physically slow her racing heart. "Of course I don't, James! But someone sneaking up on you in the dark will always be a spook!" She glared at him. "Now what the hell are we supposed to do?"

James grinned. "Let's call the Midnight Man."

Chapter Twenty

12:10 a.m.   Bedroom Camera

"I'm going to miss this," Sydney sighed, pressing a light kiss onto Charlie's neck.

The couple was stretched out on the bed, their candles set aside to create a romantic ambiance; Charlie's arm wrapped around her girlfriend's shoulders, fingers twirling her soft locks. Sydney's head was resting atop Charlie's chest, listening to the soft beat of her heart. She traced patterns into her cotton shirt, wanting to say so much but not knowing how to start. This was one of their last nights together, and the thought was causing major panic for Sydney.

"I'm going to miss you," Charlie mumbled, snuggling the top of Sydney's head. "This is one of the hardest decisions I've ever made."

Sydney shifted, searching for Charlie's eyes in the flickering light. Reflecting back was a torrent of emotions that left Sydney breathless. "Oh, Charlie," she whispered, clinging to her tighter. "Please don't let me be the one to hold you back. I'll be okay... I'll visit every weekend; I don't care about how long it takes! I promise!"

"I love you," Charlie whispered, the words choked out of her as she let the emotions overwhelm her. She tilted Sydney's face toward hers, hardly hearing the pouring of emotions as she sealed her lips with a kiss.

Chapter Twenty-One

12:12 a.m. Kitchen Camera

"Yeah, I'm pretty sure that project for drama back in freshman year was the first time I met Nikki," Whitney mused, twirling her dark hair while she reminisced. "We've been inseparable since!" She giggled, her brown eyes sparkling with the memory. "Crazy to think theatre is what brought everyone together!"

Alex pulled himself on top of the counter. "That's true. Nikki got me to join when I asked her to drive me home," he smirked. "Guess she's the one who actually got all of us together. Crazy to think, huh? I was always so shy until she forced me to join theatre. Granted, I stuck to the lighting booth, but she made sure I was at every cast party!" He grabbed a handful of pretzels from the nearby bowl and stuffed them into his mouth.

"Wait!" Whitney gasped, yanking at his wrist.

"What?" Alex froze, mouth still full.

Whitney froze too, glancing quickly around the kitchen, moving her candle to peer into the shadowy corners. "Are we allowed to eat? Did the rules say anything about food?"

"Oh my God, Whitney! You scared me half to death, I thought you saw something!" Alex admonished after swallowing. "There's nothing in the rules about snacks! No lights and no leaving!"

"That's right, sorry!" Whitney giggled nervously, twisting the same strand of hair a bit tighter this time. "I know this is all probably just a silly party game, but..."

Alex smirked. "What if it's not?"

Whitney shrugged, refusing to meet his eye. "What time is it anyway?"

Alex glanced at the stove, but the bright green numbers were no longer glowing. "Wait... did the power go out?"

Before Whitney could answer, a blood-curdling scream erupted from the basement.

Chapter Twenty-Two

12:15 a.m.   Living Room Camera

"Remember when Mr. Cost fell asleep right in the middle of the test?" Darren chuckled.

"Yes!" Nikki cried, laughing along. "I think that's the only algebra test I ever passed!" She was leaning against Darren's broad chest and was quite comfortable if she were to admit it. The two chatted about how they felt about college and then easily slipped into memories from their senior year. As they talked, his arm had slid from her shoulders to her waist, where his thumb was currently drawing circles around her hip.

"Remember Spring Break, Junior Year?" he muttered into her hair.

She giggled. "The one where you got so sunburnt everyone called you Lobster for the rest of the year?"

He huffed softly. "Ch-yeah," Darren tipped her chin up and gazed into her blue eyes. "But you have to admit, I was the best-looking lobster in the entire school."

Nikki smirked playfully. "I'm sure you cured a few girls of their shellfish allergy."

"How much longer until we rotate rooms?" He mumbled, his green eyes hinting at things to come.

It was then that both Darren and Nikki heard the scream.

Chapter Twenty-Three

12:16 a.m.   Kitchen, Handheld Camera

"Who screamed?" Charlie yelled as she and Sydney joined everyone in the kitchen, her camera swinging to the assembled faces staring intensely at the basement door.

Madicyn burst through the doorway, tears streaming down her face, her candle held in a white-knuckled fist. "It's James!" she screamed, scurrying to hide behind everyone.

"What about my brother?" Whitney asked, pulling Madicyn closer.

She took a shaky breath, wide eyes still fixed on the open basement door. "I... I told him not to," Madicyn paused to wipe her tears, but another sob bubbled up. "But he kept threatening the Midnight Man! He was shouting about how... how the Midnight Man wasn't real... and then there was this black figure... and James, I don't know..." she broke off with a sob, hiding her face.

Nikki clutched Darren's hand, curling into his frame. "What happened to him?"

Alex stepped in front of the group, his eyes looking wild in the glow of the collected candles. "Chill out everyone, this is James... I'm sure he's fine..." He glanced quickly at the camera, trembling in Charlie's hand.

"BEWARE THE MIDNIGHT MAN!"

Nikki screamed as a hulking figure emerged from the darkened doorway. It lumbered toward her, arms outstretched before finally collapsing. "Holy shit!" she cried, holding onto Darren tighter.

"James!" Whitney cried, pushing forward only for Alex to stop her with a small shake of his head. "That's my brother!" She wrenched free and kneeled next to his body.

"Oh God... is he breathing...?" Nikki detached herself from Darren and knelt next to Whitney, guiding her candle over James, searching for any signs of life.

Whitney gasped, shakily pointing toward James' face. "Is that... blood?"

Nikki leaned closer, squinting. The silence of the group created a static buzz of anticipation. Cautiously, she reached out a hand to feel for a pulse, to scan for any sign that James wasn't actually dead in front of her. Suddenly James shot up and shouted, "Boo!"

Both girls screamed and scrambled away from the now howling James. "I got you!" he kept wheezing between laughs. "Oh man, I never thought it was going to work."

"What the hell?" Nikki cried, straightening her skirt as she stood, trying to preserve whatever dignity she had left. "What is going on?"

Madicyn shared a high-five with Sydney, both girls smirking nastily at Nikki. Alex looked slightly abashed, and Charlie, to her credit, looked rather guilty. Darren was helping a still shaken Whitney to her feet.

"Come on, Nikki," Madicyn sneered. "Can't take a harmless prank?"

"Harmless?" Nikki cried. "We've been marching around in the dark, like idiots... and then you... you faked being dead? What the hell is wrong with you?"

Sydney's normally pretty face was twisted into a mask of anger. "Grow up, Nikki. We're helping Charlie, she needed footage for her freshman project. Thought you were a good friend."

"Really, bitch?" Nikki stomped toward her, only for Darren to wrap an arm around her waist, murmuring to chill out.

"Okay, prank is over!" Whitney yelled, silencing the crowd. "Let's turn the lights on now and talk this out." She flipped the wall switch, but the room remained dark. She flipped it on and off again, but there was no change. She began to flip it more frantically, but the lights didn't turn on. "Is this part of the joke?" Her voice was laced with panic.

"No," Charlie offered, "The power probably blew out from the storm... happens all the time here."

Nikki scoffed. "You sure this isn't just another scene for your stupid movie?"

"Come on, Nik," Darren took her hand, "Let's go talk somewhere until the rain slows down and then you can drive me home." Nikki rolled her eyes and stormed from the room with Darren in tow.

James continued to chuckle. "That worked out better than I thought! Hope you got some good footage, especially of my handsome mug!" He winked into the lens.

"Or my outstanding acting debut!" Madicyn giggled, striking a dramatic pose and moving her candle to illuminate her duck face.

"I do feel a little guilty," Alex admitted, glancing at Whitney, who was still huddled over her candle by the light switch. "I mean, we could have picked a simpler prank."

Madicyn rolled her eyes. "No way! This was the perfect setup! She believed the whole story about the Midnight Man!"

James wiped red goo from his face, smearing his "bloody" facade before draping an arm around her shoulders. "Maybe we can play some card games until the rain lets up? I'll grab the camera from the basement, maybe more candles?"

"Sounds good," Charlie agreed. She shifted the camera to her other hand, surveying the group. Madicyn and Sydney were sharing satisfied smiles over a prank well-played, and Alex was picking at his hoodie's zipper. "Penny for your thoughts?"

He shrugged. "I mean, it was funny, scaring them a bit..." He quickly glanced at Whitney, still silently watching her candle. "Did you get what you needed for your project?"

Charlie let out a hum. She really should talk to Nikki, apologize for scaring her. But honestly, why was she taking it so personally? Charlie shook off the echoes of an argument from years ago, when Sydney outed her on social media. Nikki was the first one to jump up to defend her. Of course, Nikki had also threatened Sydney with her fists... but the intentions were noble.

"Give her a few minutes," Alex answered Charlie's unspoken thoughts. "We'll both talk to her; I think she's just licking her wounds. She doesn't take well to embarrassment."

Charlie agreed but turned to Whitney. "You okay, Whit?" Whitney slowly lifted her gaze; tears were gathering at the corner of her eyes. "Whitney? Hey, sorry for scaring you… I mean, I can't even just blame it on James. I was just as much of an ass in this as he was…"

Whitney jerked back from Charlie's proffered hand. "We need to keep moving," she whispered, her brown eyes wild with fear. "The game is still on…"

Chapter Twenty-Four

James waited until he reached the bottom steps before pulling out his cell phone, now that the prank was over, there was no reason to continue walking blindly in the dark. He'd had years of experience giving his sister a fright, but it never ceased to amuse him, and Charlie had recorded the entire thing! He couldn't help another chuckle, imagining Nikki's face contorted in fright when he'd jumped up at her.

It was Madicyn and Sydney who suggested pulling a prank. They wanted some sort of "revenge" on Nikki, but James was in it for the laughs. He wanted to spook

Darren too, that guy was always as cool as ice... but two out of three wasn't bad, if James thought so himself.

James shivered in the basement air, tugging impatiently on the extension cord attached to the camera. Was it a universal design for basements to always be so cold? Though maybe the chill would give him an excuse to warm up a certain Ms. Madicyn. She may have had eyes for Darren, but James could tell the feelings weren't mutual.

He shone his flashlight over the camera, glancing at the array of buttons on the control panel. Shrugging, he decided it might just be easier to take the whole damn thing upstairs. *Charlie would have my hide if I, God forbid, hit the wrong button, and erased the footage already recorded,* James thought with a wry smile. Before he could detach the tripod, a flicker on the screen caught his attention.

Squinting, James tried to make heads or tails of the misshapen shadows shown in the night vision mode on the screen. It was hard to tell but... there! James swore there was movement in the corner!

"Probably just dust..." he mumbled, shining his phone's light toward the darkened space. It was so cold down there anyway; he was longing to go upstairs and warm up. "Shit!" He forgot he promised to bring extra candles.

He twisted the light to the darkened corner once more, cursing under his breath. Just as he reached the shelves, his light flickered out. "What the hell?"

Chapter Twenty-Five

I can't believe I'm making out with Darren Holt! Nikki's heart was racing; what a crazy turn of events this evening was ending up!

Darren had tugged Nikki upstairs, listening to her cursing Madicyn and Sydney. Gently, he led her into the bathroom and guided her to the counter. "Nikki," he finally cut off her tirade. "I don't care about either of them." Then he kissed her, right there in the small, cramped bathroom.

Nikki was the first one to deepen their kiss. She slid her fingers through his shaggy hair, pulling him in tighter. Madicyn wanted to embarrass her? How about this? After years of pining, Darren had finally noticed her.

Darren's hand snaked to the edge of her tank top, and Nikki could hardly suppress a shiver. Somehow, making out by candlelight made it all so much sexier.

The pair were so focused on each other, they missed the flames on their candles begin to shudder, and the muffled cries from downstairs.

Chapter Twenty-Six

12:45 a.m. Kitchen Camera

"It was just a prank, Whitney," Alex assured her, guiding her to the kitchen table. "There is no Midnight Man."

Whitney shook her head insistently. "We did the ritual!"

"It's all for fun," Sydney asserted, moving closer to Charlie. "Just a silly ghost story."

Charlie set her camera on the table, a cold trickle of doubt sliding down her spine. *They had followed the steps exactly; my blood was splashed on my name card. Was it possible? Had our joke ended with us actually summoning a demon?*

"Seriously?" Madicyn cried. "It's a dumb game we found online! What's everyone so quiet for?"

Alex scooped up the camera. "If there was anything lurking around, one of the cameras would have picked something up. Let's check them out."

Whitney rolled her candle nervously between her hands. "As long as we keep moving..."

"James!" Alex called down the basement steps. "Hurry up with that camera!"

Silence rose from the basement stairwell. Staring down the passageway, the staircase seemed to be swallowed up by the thick darkness below. Alex called down again, "James, enough already! If this is another of your pranks, I'm just going to lock you down there!" Still nothing.

"You don't think anything happened to him, do you?" Sydney asked, tightly gripping Charlie's hand.

Madicyn snorted. "Please. This is James we're talking about! He's probably waiting at the bottom of the stairs to grab one of us. Guess I'll be his next victim." She rolled her eyes as she marched toward the basement.

"I'll get Nikki and Darren," Charlie offered, already rehearsing the apology she knew her friend would be expecting.

Before Charlie had even stepped out of the room, an ear-piercing scream sounded from the basement. Madicyn clambered up the steps, her face white, eyes bulging as they searched the dark behind her.

"Madicyn?" Alex asked, catching her as she tripped over the threshold.

"His eyes!" she screeched. Madicyn continued to scootch away from the door, her breathing rapid and eyes ever fixed on the gaping darkness.

Charlie motioned for Sydney to stay behind as she inched forward, using her dim candlelight to peer into the inky black.

A face illuminated back at her, popping out of the nothingness. With unnatural, stiff steps, the figure pushed forward, his hands grasping at his throat from which rivers of blood spurted between his fingers. Charlie jumped and scrambled away.

The body let out a low, long groan before collapsing in a heap.

"James?" Whitney screamed, but Alex was holding her back. "Please!"

"Stay back!" Charlie barked. Her heart thudded wildly as she approached the body. She wished she had her phone or any other source of light other than her wildly flickering candle flame. Her voice stuck in her throat as the shadows danced around what used to be her friend. Reluctantly, she crouched closer, tilting the light to illuminate his face. His throat was torn open, the wide gash stretching off into distinctive claw marks and further up, two gaping pits stared back.

James' eyes were gone.

Chapter Twenty-Seven

1:00 a.m. Living Room Camera

"He's my brother!" Whitney was screaming, trying to tear free of Alex's stronghold as she sobbed. "Please! Let me see him!"

Alex dragged her out of the kitchen, wrestled her to the couch, and unceremoniously dumped her onto the cushions. "Whitney!" He shook her shoulders, drawing her focus onto him once again. "You don't want to see that!"

"What the hell is going on?" Madicyn demanded, storming into the living room, her face still a ghostly pale and hands still shaking violently. "What the hell happened to

James?"

Charlie and Sydney joined the group, tears streaking each of their faces. Finally, Charlie cleared her throat. "I... I'm going to get Darren and Nikki," she squeezed Sydney's hand quickly. "We all just need a minute to calm down before we discuss this."

"Calm down?" Whitney jumped up from the couch, angry red splotches staining her cheeks. "My brother is dead! His eyes are gone! How the hell am I supposed to calm down?"

Charlie held up her hand defensively. "Okay. Wrong choice of words. I've got to go upstairs to grab a sheet... to cover him up. Let's all take some deep breaths."

Sydney slid next to Whitney and wrapped her arms around her, smoothing down the wisps of black hair that escaped her tight braid and letting her sob into her shoulder. James' face haunted her; the empty pits where those mischievous chocolate eyes had once sparkled, the frozen scream of terror, the blood-caked down his cheeks... Silently, she met Alex's eyes in the candlelight. But there was just as much uncertainty there as she was feeling.

Chapter Twenty-Eight

1:05 a.m. Bathroom Camera

"You don't know how long I've wanted to do this," Darren mumbled as he kissed down Nikki's neck, inhaling her perfume.

Nikki giggled. "Probably as long as I've been fantasizing about it," she whispered in his ear, pressing him closer.

How long had they been in this bathroom? Time seemed to have slipped away from the two of them. In the dancing candlelight, there only existed the two of them. Desires manifested, and they acted upon their secret wishes.

Until the bathroom door opened with a bang.

"Dammit!" Nikki cried, adjusting her tank top to a decent spot. "Ever heard of knocking?"

Darren, too, had a hard time meeting Charlie's eyes as her accusatory glare flashed over the two of them impatiently.

"Both of you need to come downstairs. Something happened." Her words were strained as emotion and annoyance battled within her. *James was dead, and these two are... canoodling in my bathroom?*

Nikki just rolled her eyes, straightening her ponytail and coolly ignoring her friend's clear irritation. "Is this another scene for your movie? Is James going to grab me as soon as I get to the bottom of the stairs?"

"No," Charlie took a shuddering breath. "James is dead."

Chapter Twenty-Nine

1:11 a.m.   Living Room Camera

"We should call the police." Madicyn insisted, pacing in a tight circle. "There's a dead body in the kitchen... why are we just sitting here? We have to do something!"

Alex snorted softly. "What are we going to tell them? We were playing some game and then suddenly our friend lost his eyes? You really think they're going to believe us?"

"So, what's your solution, Alex? Just sit here while James rots in the next room? Your friend's corpse is in the middle of the kitchen! There is no Midnight Man!"

"Hey!" Charlie yelled as she rejoined the group, clutching a white sheet in her hands. "Yelling isn't going to solve anything. We have to try to keep cool and figure this out."

"C'mon, Charlie," Sydney muttered, "I'll help you cover him up."

Nikki swooped down and embraced Whitney, whispering apologies for her absence. When she pulled back, she was suddenly self-conscious of the stares of scrutiny from the room's occupants. "Um, can anyone explain what happened?"

Alex shifted uncomfortably. "We're not quite sure. James went downstairs to get the camera and... well, when he came back up... his eyes and throat were gouged out."

"You don't think it was..."

"The Midnight Man?" Madicyn cut in. "Grow up! It's just a ghost story. None of it is real!"

Sydney came back into the room, cell phone in hand. "I'm going to call the police. We can't just have a dead body sitting in my kitchen all night!"

"Wait!" Whitney called, nervously watching Sydney's fingers dance across the screen. "You can't use your phone! It's against the rules!"

"Really, Whitney?" Sydney's voice cracked. "That's your brother! What else do you want me to do?" She continued to dial the number.

Whitney shuddered as if chilled. "The game isn't over," she insisted.

Sydney jabbed at the screen with an irritated huff. "Busy signal," she muttered. *How could the phone line to the police be jammed? Were that many people calling in because of the storm?* "What is it, babe?" she asked, turning to Charlie.

Charlie looked up as she slid the sheet over James' face. "I didn't say anything?"

"I swear, I just heard you say my name..." she muttered, turning away again. "I'm not getting through." She gestured helplessly to her phone.

"I'll try it," Nikki offered, grabbing the proffered device.

"Charlie? Did you need something?" Sydney turned, pacing closer to the kitchen island, but saw Charlie was already heading back to the living room.

"Babe?" Charlie asked, concerned. "I didn't say anything…"

That's when Sydney's candle went out.

Chapter Thirty

1:20 a.m.   Handheld Camera

"Re-light it!" Charlie yelled, rushing forward over the kitchen threshold with a lighter. "Quick!"

Sydney's hands shook as she flicked the lighter's tiny wheel. "I... I can't...!" Her face drained to a deathly pale, her hands trembling as she desperately tried to produce a flame. "My lighter isn't working!"

"She has the votive candle! Who has the twin? My candle can't reach the wick!" Charlie cried out as she desperately tried to maneuver her flame to catch the wick.

Sydney visibly paled. "James had the other votive..."

"Salt!" Darren cried out, digging in his pocket for the small baggie. "Salt is supposed to protect you!"

"Right!" Alex agreed. "Draw a ring of salt around you, and you're safe!"

Sydney complied, spilling a wide, shaky circle before releasing a heavy sigh. The friends waited in tense silence, waiting desperately for something... anything to happen.

Finally, Madicyn stepped forward, her face screwed up in a tight pout. "This is ridiculous!" She stamped her foot. "A ring of salt? What the hell is that supposed to do. This isn't real!"

"Chill out, Madicyn," Darren growled. His whole body was tense as he glared at her. "What more proof do you need that this is much more than some game?"

Madicyn rolled her eyes. "Oh please," she flipped her dark hair over her shoulder. Her gaze burned with a jealous fire. "Like it wasn't totally obvious Nikki blew out the candle?"

Sydney shifted within her confined space. "I did feel a breeze…"

"Really?" Nikki asked sarcastically, surveying the group's expressions. "Do you really think I'd sacrifice Sydney to a demon?"

"There is no demon!" Madicyn screamed.

"Please!" Whitney's sob broke off any other argument. "My brother is dead!" She cried out. Her face was blotchy, and her eyes swollen as tears continued to rush down her cheeks. "Please… let's just get through the night."

"We only have a few more hours," Alex offered. "Let's split up again. We'll shift rooms every half hour."

Nikki and Darren grasped hands. Madicyn rolled her eyes at the pair. "I guess I'll be the one to go solo. I'll take upstairs."

"I'm staying with Sydney," Charlie announced.

"Nikki and I will go to the basement," Darren stated.

Nikki shivered and grasped his hand tighter. "But Darren, James just got attacked in the basement, I don't know if that's the best place to investigate…"

Darren's warm, dark eyes met hers. "You're right, Nik. That's why we have to go down there, try to see if we can get any sort of clue. We're doing it for James!"

Nikki's face conveyed a lack of assurance, but she offered no protest.

Whitney wiped her tears away and sniffled softly. "Guess you're stuck with me." She gave Alex a watery smile.

"No problem, Whit," He smiled back. "We'll just be in the living room."

With grim nods, the group split up.

Chapter Thirty-One

1:30 a.m.   Basement Camera

"You had to choose the basement?" Nikki whined, curling closer to Darren.

Darren's eyes stayed trained on the surrounding dark, his body was tense and ready for confrontation. "This is completely insane," he muttered.

Nikki held her candle closer. "I'm scared," she whispered. "I... I can't believe what happened to James... and now Sydney is stuck..." Her words caught in her throat.

Darren's arms wrapped around her, pulling Nikki flush against him. "I promise, I will protect you."

Nikki's heart raced at his assuredness. "Even against... well, whatever sort of supernatural being this is?"

"Yes, Nikki. I promise, I won't let him get you. Ever."

Chapter Thirty-Two

1:35 a.m.   Living Room Camera

"Tell me more about this Midnight Man?" Whitney asked softly.

Alex snapped out of his stupor, examining his friend's shadowy features. She had stopped crying, but her normally lively brown eyes were dull and lifeless. With the reflection of the flames, her skin appeared sickly, and the dark circles under her eyes impossibly deep. The living room, painted a cheery yellow, now looked sallow in the darkness and made Alex feel disconcerted. Shifting uncomfortably in his seat, his eyes scanned the room, as if merely speaking his name would cause him to appear. "Uhm... I don't really..."

"Please, Alex," Whitney begged. "I just want to know what we're up against.

Alex fidgeted with the frayed sleeve of his hoodie, his eyes avoiding Whitney's as he tried to frame his story. His candle's flame flickered with his heavy sigh. "Well... Charlie wanted to film some things from the party; a memento for when she was away... I thought it might be fun to play a game."

Whitney didn't comment, but her stare remained intensely focused on Alex; her knuckles white against her candle.

"Remember how fun *Bloody Mary* was when we were kids? I thought maybe if we found some other spooky game, it'd really spice up the film. Of course, Sydney wanted in... and somehow Madicyn and James were pulled in too... it turned into a prank on Nikki along the way..." He paused, his gaze following the shadows cast by the flickering flames. "The Midnight Game sounded simple enough... and terrifying. Countless videos and blogs and forums were dedicated to this elusive Midnight Man."

"What did they say?" Whitney whispered.

Alex shrugged. "Honestly, it sounded like your typical horror movie garbage. I sifted through almost every website and read all the blogs and testimonials that were available. Some claimed the game was a hoax... others had much more gruesome tales; hallucinations of their worst fears, time loops, torture... really sick things."

Whitney visibly shuddered. "So why did you want to go through with this?"

"Curiosity?" Alex felt a guilty blush creep up his neck. "I've always had a morbid fascination for these types of things... and this sounded truly scary."

"It was for your vlog, wasn't it?" Whitney's voice was cold. "You wanted it to be real... so you could have something to post."

Alex gaped back at her, the denial dying before it passed his lips. He couldn't lie to Whitney, not when her brother's corpse grew cold in the room next to them. Alex had initially agreed to this Game first to make Charlie happy and then selfishly because he did want it to be real. He wanted the fear to be tangible enough that it'd translate well through the lens. Something to really set their little vlog over the edge. Never had he imagined it'd end in murder.

Whitney brushed her long braid over her shoulder; a dark look had overtaken her features, wedging a frosty distance between the two. "Well, Alex... you got your wish. I hope you don't have to pay for it."

Chapter Thirty-Three

1:45 a.m. Bathroom Camera

"I don't know why I'm doing this," Madicyn perched on the edge of the toilet lid, adjusting the tripod and camera to center herself in the frame. "This is so typical, James choosing the bathroom for something that's supposed to be heartfelt." She fidgeted with her candle rolling it between her hands. "I... I can't believe he's dead..."

Madicyn had always prided herself on keeping a hard exterior. She was cool, confident, poised in every situation. She had dreams of being a reporter on a news station, wearing pressed suits and sipping strong coffee every morning as she laid out the day's top stories. There were very few she let into her vulnerabilities, to see what was under the carefully constructed mask. Charlie had been the first one, she was also confident but also laid back and open. Madicyn had a feeling Charlie's qualities as a leader were natural, unlike her own facade of being cool and in control. Charlie had introduced her to James, and he rocked Madicyn's entire world with his wit and sarcasm, shaking the solid ground she had built for herself.

"I just can't admit it was a demon that killed him," Madicyn continued. "That's absolutely ridiculous. I don't have an explanation for what happened, but let's be real. The Midnight Man took his eyes? This is a game Alex found on the internet, not anything real." Tears pricked at her eyes. "James was a good friend, and I can't accept that some paranormal force killed him. He deserves better than that." She sniffled.

James forced cracks in her exterior. He challenged her to really evaluate her choices. How many times had James called her out for her attitude? Sure, Madicyn acted like a bitch... but only when people deserved it. She broke up with Darren because of late-night talks with James, questioning why she was still with a guy she clearly had moved on from. And tonight... he pulled her aside and accused her of throwing herself at Darren just because Nikki was interested.

"James was so insightful," Madicyn confessed to the camera, her gaze flicking between the lens and the flame, watching the dancing patterns manifesting. "I think he knew me better than I even know myself." She choked on the emotion. "I dated Darren on and off throughout high school... four years with the same guy and Darren never thought to ask the questions James did. He never really saw me. Darren... he wanted to be the dream couple, sure. And he's really not a bad guy... but he wasn't James."

Madicyn let the tears fall, leaving salty streaks in their wake. She wept for what she missed out on, for what could have been if she hadn't been so stubborn, and she wept for her friend growing cold on the kitchen floor.

"This whole thing is stupid," Madicyn declared, the hard edge returning to her voice. She irritatingly wiped away what was left of her tears. Digging in the pockets of her skinny jeans, she pulled out her cell phone. "I'm calling the 9-1-1. We have to get through to them eventually."

Madicyn only got as far as punching in her password before she felt heat consume the left side of her face. The small flame of her candle had exploded into a ball of angry fire and leaped to her hair. Her skull was burning, crackling against her perfectly styled locks. With a shriek, Madicyn flung her phone and scrambled to the sink, dunking her head under the faucet and turning on the icy water.

The heat grew more intense, scorching the back of her neck and consuming the entirety of her scalp. "Why isn't the water working?" She screamed. Why was she still burning? The popping and sizzling in her ear drowned out her own screams. Madicyn kept her head under the spray, praying the flames would fizzle out. She groped for a towel to douse the flames, but the heat became too much. Just as she felt her knees weaken and her senses dull from the white-hot pain, Madicyn felt a phantom hand grip her neck and shove her under the icy stream, and a deep cackle echoed around her.

Jerking back, Madicyn caught her expression in the mirror. Her perfectly contoured face was a mess of makeup running down her now ghost-white face, her hair matted and dripping but... not singed.

Leaning closer to the mirror, Madicyn examined the reflection, her hair was fine. Bringing a lock to her nose, she sniffed but found no evidence of ever having been on fire in the first place.

Hands shaking, Madicyn lifted her candle, and other than the dripping wax had no other indication of the molten weapon it had become. Madicyn's eyes slid to the camera, blinking in confusion. She cautiously glanced at her phone screen, illuminating it with a few soft taps. The displayed numbers confirmed a half hour had passed and it was time to move on. She took a deep, shaky breath, reconstructing her mask of cold indifference. After using a washcloth to clean up her makeup mess, she scurried from the bathroom without a backward glance.

Chapter Thirty-Four

1:55 a.m. Kitchen Camera

"What time is it now?" Sydney asked, giving her blonde hair an impatient tug.

Charlie waved the question aside. "It doesn't matter, babe. I'm here. We're going to get through this." *Thank God the power is still out*, Charlie thought, *at least Sydney doesn't have to see how agonizingly slow the minutes are oozing by.*

Sydney rolled her eyes. "You're not the one stuck in this circle." She pouted. *Why me? I'd much rather be wrapped in Charlie's arms... much like Nikki and Darren were in the basement, I bet.*

Charlie reached over the salt barrier and squeezed her girlfriend's hand. "I'd rather know you were safe here than..." She couldn't stop her eyes from darting over to where James' body lay under the sheet. A shudder coursed through her. "He can't get you here, all the stories online said so."

"Stories... Charlie, are we even sure this is real?"

"Syd, seriously? You heard him calling your name... you can see James is missing his eyes! His throat is just a gaping hole! These aren't just coincidences."

Sydney bit her lip, feeling her anxiety threaten to overtake her. It was so much easier to explain it all away as a prank gone terribly wrong. Nikki trying to get payback on them, James taking his joke too far and getting hurt... but she couldn't lie to herself. She had felt the icy fingers dig into her shoulder, heard the rattling voice as it whispered her name. Even now, beyond her circle and the safety of Charlie's flame, she could almost discern a shape darting in the shadows, just waiting for her to leave her sodium sanctuary.

Charlie's hand wrapped around Sydney's, fingers intertwining in the familiar,

comfortable way the two shared. The
gesture acted as the anchor Sydney needed,
pulling her away from the dark thoughts
threatening to drown her in their madness.
If... no, when they got through this, Sydney
determined, *I am going to do everything in
my power to show Charlie we were destined
to be together. Maybe even move to that
college town I had so vehemently hoped
Charlie would not choose.*

"Ok, love birds... break it up, half hour
is over." Madicyn was leaning against the
doorway, a smirk on her face as she casually
tapped the base of her candle.

Charlie squinted, raising her candle to
shine more light toward Madicyn. "Were
you... crying?"

Madicyn's face fell for a moment, and
a rare glimpse of panic shone before she
quickly replaced her cold expression. "No, it's
just a trick of this dim lighting."

Sydney smiled encouragingly. "It's
okay, Madicyn. We know you were close to
James." She noticed Madicyn refused to look
at either of them. "Is... is your hair wet?"

Madicyn shook her mane of dark hair
behind her, her cheeks flushing. "Seriously,

all you have is a candle for light, I'm fine. Besides, it's time to rotate. It's my turn in here."

"We're splitting up?" Nikki and Darren had just come up from the basement. She clung to Darren's hand tighter, the thought of not having him next to her made her heart race.

"I'll partner with you, Nikki," Whitney offered, not giving Alex a second glance.

"Why don't we stick to the basement?" Nikki asked.

Whitney stiffened. "My brother died down there!"

Nikki grasped her friend's hand. "I'm here for you, Whit. We can face this together so you can confront this and move on! Trust me, I was scared going down there too, but being with Darren soothed my fears. Being together, it's not nearly as bad!"

"I'm not sure that's how it works," Whitney muttered. She peered into the gaping darkness of the open doorway. "Are you sure that counts as moving? Can you go back to the basement without breaking the movement rule?"

"I don't see why not? I'm up here now, right?" With a reluctant sigh, Nikki gestured to the dark steps and let her friend pass. She paused before following, her eyes locking with Darren. He leaned close and whispered a promise of their reunion before kissing her tightly.

Madicyn rolled her eyes at the display, not trying to hide her bitter expression. "I'll stay with Sydney."

"Come on, Charlie... we'll go upstairs. Darren, looks like you're solo in the living room." Alex offered, shifting the handheld camera to pan across the assembled group. "Only an hour and a half left, guys."

Chapter Thirty-Five

2:03 a.m. Bedroom Camera

"I feel so guilty leaving her alone down there..." Charlie whispered, settling herself on the bed. She leaned against the headboard and let her eyes sink shut. She pictured Sydney's wide eyes pleading with her not to abandon her. "Is this my torture?" She mumbled, brushing her palm across the flickering flame.

Alex glanced up from his camera, anything to avoid admitting to Charlie; he too, was drowning in guilt. His friends were suffering, and he was the root of the problem. *If I hadn't been so damn selfish, wanting to get that perfect shot...* his hands shook at the thought. "We didn't have a choice. Sydney understands, we had to move on, or you'd be in your own circle right now."

"Or worse..." Charlie locked eyes with Alex. His face was grim, his eyes mournful behind his precisely placed dark bangs. "Do you think..."

Alex held up his hand. "Don't, Charlie. I don't even want to go there. We're going to make it out of this. People have survived this game before, we've read about it."

Charlie watched as he trained the camera back on her, heard the whir as the lens zoomed in on her dark expression. Her thoughts whirled in a violent storm, a constant beat of the message that her friends were suffering because of her; the reminder of the less than optimistic posts she'd read from "survivors." A shiver coursed down her spine as she recalled a particular article about a girl who was so terrified after the game she was admitted to an asylum. At the time, Charlie and Alex both laughed at how ridiculous it sounded. But now? Now she just longed to stroke Sydney's hair one more time; to keep her safe from whatever was stalking them.

Chapter Thirty-Six

2:20 a.m.   Kitchen Camera

"I still think this is a bunch of bullshit," Madicyn moaned, brushing a final layer of nail polish on her toes. Though the puffiness around her eyes had finally gone down, she still felt the salty tracks of her tears. "It's a dumb game Charlie and Alex found on the Internet," she continued, refusing to admit, even to Sydney, what she'd experienced in the bathroom. "We're just convincing ourselves it's supernatural."

Sydney gave a noncommittal hum, giving her own nails a quick touch up of polish. It was easy for Madicyn to brush the experiences off as just a game, she wasn't the one stuck in a ring of salt on the cold kitchen tile. She wondered how much more time they had before this was over.

Madicyn stood and stretched. "I'm going to mix myself a drink. Do you want anything?" After hearing Sydney's polite decline, she measured out a good portion of vodka into a Solo cup and took a generous swig. Anything to warm this sudden chill she was enveloped in. She shivered and quickly masked it with another gulp of vodka. She glanced at her phone screen; they had just over an hour before this dumb charade was over. She scoffed at the very idea that some demon was chasing them around the house.

"Mads!" Sydney squeaked. Her face was drained of color, and her eyes wide with terror as she stared at her friend.

Madicyn was confused at the sudden change in mood when she followed Sydney's shaking finger to her candle. A wisp of smoke curling from the wick, the flame suddenly extinguished. *Shit, what was the rule? Ten seconds?* She fumbled in her pockets but realized her lighter was missing. *Dammit! Where had I tossed it?*

"Draw a circle of salt!" Sydney shrieked. "Or jump into mine! Anything to protect yourself!"

"Shut up, Syd!" Madicyn growled as she groped around the counter for the small Bic. "I told you, there's no such thing as the Midnight Man! I'm not going to wander around this damn cold house in the dark, though!" Finally finding the lighter, she flicked the wheel and relit her candle. There was a tense second as the two girls scanned the dark corners of the kitchen. Madicyn smirked and raised her cup. "See? Nothing to worry about! Cheers, Midnight Man!" She tipped it back and finished the burning liquid, relishing in the victory of knowing there really weren't any beings chasing them down.

Upon lowering the cup, Madicyn's sneer of triumph faded. Nikki stood in the doorway of the basement with a grim expression, her blue eyes devoid of their normal spark. "Bad girl, Madicyn..." she whispered.

Madicyn rolled her eyes. "Whatever, slut. You're the one who stole Darren from me." She scowled. "I see you've abandoned your candle; have you finally come to your senses and realized this game is just a crock of shit?"

Nikki began moving forward, seeming to flicker in and out of focus, always glitching closer and closer across the tiles, all the while her eyes remained locked on to Madicyn. "You never follow the rules, Madicyn. The rules must be obeyed."

"What the hell are you talking about?" Madicyn felt a tingle at the back of her neck, as if a finger were slowly tracing her vertebrae.

"Bad girls who don't follow the rules must face their consequences," Nikki whispered. She appeared right in front of Madicyn, her breath an icy gust on Madicyn's cheeks.

Madicyn shoved Nikki back. "Stay away from me!"

Nikki grabbed a clump of Madicyn's curls and dragged her across the floor. Madicyn clawed at the hand tangled in her hair, screaming for its release. Nikki kept repeating in an eerie chant, "Break the rules, face the consequences."

Madicyn's head was slammed against the counter, her hair yanked hard enough that she was forced to train her eyes on Nikki. Nikki was grinning maniacally down at her and releasing small gleeful giggles. "Let's wash that pretty mouth out, Madicyn."

With an animal growl, Madicyn fought back against the iron-clad hold on her head. She heard the faucet begin, felt the icy splash against her face as Nikki dragged her closer to the stream. Madicyn always thought Nikki was crazy, but now she was trying to kill her? She tried to sweep Nikki's feet from under her only to be met with a "tsk-tsk."

"Oh, Madicyn... so brave, so perfect. But never good enough. Pretty enough to catch the boy's eye but not enough to keep it. Sweet enough to be the friend but not enough to be the first one invited in on the plan."

Madicyn let out a sob. Nikki's grip was too much, her scalp was burning! Suddenly, her face was forced under the water, feeling it stream into her nose, into her mouth... there was no escape from the roar and needles of the icy water. Desperately she clawed at the iron grip holding her hair. Just when she thought she couldn't take any more, her head was removed from the spray and slammed against the marble counter again.

Nikki's head was cocked at an impossible angle, her mouth stretched into a grin crossing her entire face. "You hide yourself behind all these layers... let's see what's under this face, shall we?" Nikki slid open a drawer under the counter and brandished a potato peeler from the depths. "We'll peel back every carefully constructed layer until we see the real you."

In the distance, Madicyn thought she heard someone scream her name, but it was drowned out by her own shrieking. Just as the peeler slipped under her skin and began to hack the skin from the muscle, making small wet noises with each chunk of flesh leaving her face, Madicyn's vision blurred, melting away Nikki's maniacal face to reveal a much darker, less human shadow in its place. The entity posing as Nikki leaned close, "So glad we were able to get that nasty first layer off, I heard true beauty lies within. Let's see if that old saying is true, huh?" She dangled what looked like a thin piece of lunch meat before her, flicking it into the sink with a sticky slap. Nikki licked the thick blood from her fingers before winking and diving in again. Before Madicyn could scream for help, everything faded to black.

Chapter Thirty-Seven

2:20 a.m. Basement Camera

"I hate this, I hate everything about this!" Nikki shivered, rubbing the gooseflesh covering her arm. She clutched her candle tight, noting that it had already diminished half the wax since they began this twisted game. "I keep dreaming of my warm bed, the fluffy blankets..." She paused, noting Whitney's distance expression. "I'm sorry," she murmured. "How are you holding up?"

Whitney's soft sigh caused her small flame to flicker dangerously. "Do you think this is some sort of divine punishment?"

"What?" Nikki's face scrunched in disbelief. "Whitney, the only thing we're being punished for is being stupid enough to summon a demon. It was foolish. But we'll survive..."

"You think so?" Whitney cocked her head to the side, considering. "Alex feels personally responsible for all this, you know. He knew the potential risk and just decided to sacrifice us all in the hopes of getting a decent scene for his... whatever the hell he calls it." Her voice had taken a bitter edge. "My brother's corpse is rotting upstairs all for his stupid prank!"

Nikki reached out gently for her friend's shoulder. But Whitney lashed out with her candle, wildly. "It was about you!" Whitney's voice was low, her eyes wide, and the pupils slowly expanding. "They wanted to get back at you."

The already chilly air of the basement turned frosty. Nikki felt the cold seep into her very core. Nervously, she licked at her suddenly parched lips. *My fault? How could Whitney possibly be blaming me?* "Whit, come on... you sound positively crazy!"

A choked noise somewhere between a laugh and a sob croaked from Whitney. "You're right! I am crazy! Crazy terrified of the evil being stalking us in this damn house!

And we're playing his game. It's just a matter of time before he picks us off one by one... 'cause where are we going to go? And what's gonna save us? Salt?" She whipped out her bag from her pocket, dangling it playfully. "I don't know about you, but I don't feel too safe with it." She carelessly threw it over her shoulder.

"Stop it, Whitney!" Nikki screeched, tears pricking her eyes. Nikki was just as scared as Whitney, but in order to survive, they had to keep their cool. "Let's go back upstairs, there's really no reason to be split up."

"Why? So you can make out with your boyfriend again?" Whitney's usually serene features were twisted into a nasty sneer, the candlelight casting sinister shadows to her face. A particularly icy breeze whipped past them, and Whitney let out a howl. "I've always stood up for you, Nikki! Always! I only came to this damn party because I figured James and his friends would plan something... and look where that got me!"

Nikki sniffled. "What are you saying, Whitney?"

The girls glared at each other in the flickering lights. Their candles were protectively guarded close, and their opposite hands curled into fists. Though Nikki's face was streaked with tears, her features were determined. Whitney's face too, showed a cold fury. The standoff ended when they were both plunged into darkness as their candles simultaneously spluttered out.

Chapter Thirty-Eight

2:28 a.m. Bathroom Camera

"It's real! It's all real!" Sydney sobbed, frantically flicking the light switch with no luck. She double-checked the lock on the door before sinking to the floor, covering her face in an attempt to stifle her whimpers.

What the hell just happened down there? One-minute Madicyn was drinking, and the next, she was screaming about Nikki and then... Sydney shuddered. Watching Madicyn being bent over the counter and forced to carve off her own face by a phantom force while she was stuck in her sodium confines, only offering screams to snap her out of whatever haze she was in proved ineffectual.

Sydney wiped at her face with the back of her hand, only smearing the salty tracks on her cheeks. With a teary sniffle, she crawled over to the bathtub. Removing the camera from the tripod, she trained it on her face.

"Charlie," she croaked. Clearing her throat, she took a deep breath to center herself and try again. "Charlie... I know you're going to find this recording because you're going to survive." Sydney attempted a smile, but her muscles merely gave a weak twitch before completely settling on a grimace. "I should have said this so long ago... but I should never have said anything all those years ago. I'm sorry I wasn't strong enough to admit I had feelings for you. You remember how my dad was when he was still alive! He was always so involved in the church, and he loved his parish... the parish that caused Mom to leave us. She used to call them hens." Sydney sniffed and even managed a watery smile. "They would always be clucking away after service, and Mom warned me to always be my best, to not give them any reason to whisper about us." A sob choked her. "But clearly, I was incapable of that because Mom left anyway. It broke Dad, so I have strived to be a daughter he could be proud of." She took a shaky breath and tried to brush off her tears. "I wanted to be a teacher like Mom, but I want to teach chemistry for the challenge. Dad loved that..."

Sydney paused her rant when she thought she heard footsteps shuffling along the carpet outside. Straining her hearing, she was only met by static silence.

Refocusing on the camera, Sydney felt fresh tears prick at her eyes. "I'm sorry, Charlie. I love you... I think I fell for you the moment I met you. You were always so confident, you were a natural leader, always talking up a crowd and getting everyone psyched. It's a gift, Charlie. It's why you'll make a great director." A sob threatened to break free, and Sydney cleared her throat to dispel it. "I just wanted to make you happy," all she could manage was a whisper. "My whole life I've felt like I was lost... I was so worried about disappointing people I followed their lead, even if it meant losing a piece of myself. You saved me, Charlie. I didn't have to be pulled in all those directions anymore... you were the one who'd set me right."

Once again, the sound of deliberate steps made Sydney pause. But with all her focus on the sound, she heard nothing.

"I love you, Charlie. And I'm sorry I couldn't be stronger." She blew a kiss at the lens and sloppily reattached the camera to the tripod.

"Sydney, please!"

Sydney gasped as she heard Madicyn's terrified scream, muffled by the door. "Mads?" She called shakily. *No, she reasoned, I saw Madicyn's body lying limp in the sink... she's dead.*

"Babe? Open up, please..." Charlie's voice this time.

Another sob ripped from her throat. "I'm scared! I need you, Charlie!" Sydney gasped.

The doorknob rattled. "Unlock the door, Syd. Let me in..."

Sydney paused, her fingers hovering over the lock. Sure, the voice sounded like Charlie's initially... but there was something decidedly off about it. Almost as if there were a faint distortion in the tone.

The knob rattled again, a bit more violently than before. "Syd, it's me... let me in!"

Sydney's hand grasped her mouth as if whatever was claiming to be her girlfriend wouldn't hear her erratic breathing.

"Sydney, let me in!" This time it was Madicyn's voice, panicked. There was loud knocking on the door. "Please, Syd! Before he gets me! Don't let me die!"

The two voices melded together, blending into a scream of her name, begging for the door to be unlocked. The pounding increased, an incessant drumbeat ricocheting in her mind.

Sydney screwed her eyes shut, her hands clawing at her hair, squeezing her ears and chanted through grit teeth, "Go away, go away... please go away!"

And it all stopped. The only sound that remained was Sydney's heavy breathing. She dared to crack her eye open and stared at the blank pink walls through a bleary haze of tears. She hesitated for a tense minute of silence, allowing the thuc of her heartbeat to slow in anticipation. Just as she gave one last, pitiful sniffle, the click of the bathroom door's lock echoed in the static quiet.

Sydney huddled in the corner next to the toilet, the tile floor seeping their iciness into her veins as she watched the door slowly swing open.

Her screams were cut short when the door slammed shut.

Chapter Thirty-Nine

2:28 a.m. Handheld Camera

"Why won't the door open?" Charlie screamed, slamming her hand against the bedroom door. She frantically twisted at the doorknob only to meet resistance.

Alex kept the camera trained on her, trying to steady his hands. "Charlie, you're just wearing yourself out. Take a deep breath and wait on the bed, let me take a crack at it."

Her eyes, brimming with unshed tears of frustration, glowed a menacing green in the candle's weak flame. "Turn that damn camera off! This isn't a game, Alex!" Charlie swiftly kicked the unmoving door. "Don't tell me you didn't hear that? That was Sydney screaming! She needs me!" She began clawing at the wood, animalistic howls escaping her as she continued to fail.

"Charlie!" Alex roared, wrestling with his friend to try to restrain her wrists. Already she had scraped her fingernails to the bit, slivers of wood sticking through her raw fingers from her desperation. "James and Sydney are my friends too! You don't think it's not eating me alive that all this suffering is because of me? Don't you remember all those forums we read? This is all the Midnight Man! He's messing with us! He can make us hallucinate our greatest fears, possess us to turn on one another, relive our worst nightmares! Don't let him win, Charlie. Please, I can't lose you too..."

Charlie's lip quivered, her eyes unfocused in a mad, wide-eyed stare. "Sydney always joked about my hero complex... I can't save her Alex..." Her voice broke, and she sank into the carpet, gripping it as if she'd fall through the floor at any moment.

Alex knelt next to her, offering a supportive hand on her shoulder. They both stiffened when they heard the distant scream seeming to echo down the hallway.

Chapter Forty

2:28 a.m. Basement Camera

"Whitney..." Nikki's voice cracked, her hand shaking when the wick finally took to the lighter's flame. Straining against the shadows seeming to thicken and choke her, she turned in a tight circle, squinting to make out her friend past the weak glow. "Were you able to form a salt circle?"

A sniffle from the left caught her attention. Tiptoeing, Nikki stretched her candle out past its protective cradle against her chest. She shrieked at the sudden movement across her foot, just a centipede scuttling into the inky corners.

"Nikki..." Whitney's whisper was a mere rattle only a foot from where Nikki stood. The wispy flame seemed to pull toward her hunched frame, illuminating brown eyes with pupils dilated and gaping, seeing beyond the dusty basement walls. Whitney's hands were clawing at her face, tangling in her hair and ripping at her braid. Her skin, once so rich in color, had paled to a milky gray. Suddenly, her arm snapped out and locked on to Nikki's wrist. "Where's your bravado now?"

In vain, Nikki struggled, trying to yank her arm away. "Please, Whitney! We're best friends, Whitney! Let me go!"

Whitney's nails curled into the soft flesh, a throaty chuckle bubbling up. "Oh Nikki, what a friend you are! So worried about your hair, your makeup... who's looking at you. You've written quite the narrative for yourself, haven't you?" Whitney pulled Nikki against her, using her free arm to snake around to the back pocket of her denim skirt. "Ah! Here it is!" She slipped Nikki's compact mirror out of the pocket. "I know you always keep it close, right?"

"Whitney," Nikki sobbed. "What's happening to you?"

"You wouldn't know! Would you Nikki? Whitney never had anything juicy enough for you to be involved in... she was always so worried about you, but you never even noticed, did you? So... she let me in because she needed a friend..." That throaty chuckle again.

"You're stronger than this! Don't let him get to you!" Whitney's nails dug deeper into her wrist, breaking the skin and burning her flesh. With a scream, Nikki swung her free arm to deliver a solid right hook to her friend's jaw, connecting with a satisfying crack.

A mixture of a howl and a scream of laughter ripped from Whitney. "Nikki, Nikki," she sing-songed, her voice much rougher than its usual melodious tone. "Nikki who trusts, Nikki who loves... Nikki who would do anything for her friends." Her tongue snaked out and lapped at the blood on her fingertips, a smirk slipping on her lips. "Nikki, so wrapped up in being the perfect friend, she didn't care who was left in her wake. And Whitney? What about boring, plain Whitney? The shadow of all her friends, but when left alone where does she stand?" Whitney began crawling toward Nikki, her head arching unnaturally to maintain her hypnotic stare. "Bottom of the ladder."

Nikki backed away, her sobs clogging midway through her throat and choking her. "Let her go," she croaked. "She's my best friend, I'm sorry! I... I didn't mean to ignore her! I'm the one who should be punished!"

Another throaty cackle as Whitney continued to slither toward her. "Don't worry, Nikki," she crooned. "You'll be punished too."

Nikki felt cold hands wrap around her arms, holding her in place as a gust of frosty air twisted around her frame. She watched in horror as her weak flame spluttered out once again, and Whitney's twisted form plunged into dark. She felt pain sharp as nails sank into her ankles and yanked her to the concrete, her head smashing against the cold beneath her. Whitney rolled on top of her, skin so translucent she was more shadow than flesh and bone. Nikki wriggled underneath her, managing to throw her off. She made a mad scramble for the staircase.

"Where are you going, best friend?" Rasped in Nikki's ear before an icy grip dug into her shoulder and threw her against the heavy shelving units in the corner. With a solid thud, several glass figures fell from above and smashed around her. Covering her eyes, Nikki spun away only to smash into an ornate mirror resting against the unit. Nikki lost her balance and slipped among the shards with a shriek, her head bouncing against the concrete. With no strength to even crawl away, Whitney straddled her, knees digging sharply into her hips. Nikki gave another pathetic wiggle to try to buck the weight off of her, but her attempts were halted by the burning stab into her back. She screamed and tried to claw at the being on top of her, but another shard was twisted into her flesh.

Her vision was blurry, and her body had all but gone completely numb from the impact, but Nikki could still feel Whitney's icy fingers caress her cheek and feel her breath in her ear as she whispered, "Best friends until the end, right Nik?"

Chapter Forty-One

2:33 a.m. Handheld Camera

"We only have an hour left, Charlie. Just sixty minutes left of this nightmare, and then it's over." Alex coaxed, warily eyeing his friend.

Charlie stared at the door without any recognition that Alex had spoken, as if her gaze alone would unlock it. So far, the Midnight Man hadn't seemed intimidated by their pathetic attempts, and they'd both long since ceased their screaming and clawing at the wood. Listlessly, Charlie fiddled with the knobs on the handheld camera, changing the night mode setting to intensify the contrast and making Alex's eyes two glowing white pools in the greyscale world on the screen.

"What does that mean, Alex?" She didn't bother looking up, and instead, trained her observations on the white voids in the screen. "Will the nightmare be over? Wasn't that the clause on one of the websites we read? We'll have to relive our nightmares over and over again in some endless loop..." This time her eyes met his, the sheen of tears glinting in the dim lighting. "I don't think I'll ever rid myself of the screaming."

Alex tried to think of some comforting words, some sort of assurance that Sydney was fine, their friends were okay, and they'd find solace in surviving the night together. But the same invincible force holding the door shut also swallowed his words.

"Quite the prank, huh?" she whispered.

"Are you guys okay?" The door was flung open to reveal Darren, his face ashen housing wide-eyes and on top, a disheveled mass of hair. His hands shook as his gaze darted wildly around the room as if he suspected the Midnight Man to be looming around the corner.

Charlie was on her feet, flinging the camera aside to capture the two in an askew angle in the doorway. Her hands gripped his t-shirt tightly, her knuckles white in desperation. "Where's Sydney?"

Darren gaped at Charlie, attempting to disentangle himself from her. "She... she ran past me, practically flew up the stairs. I tried to call out to her, to follow her, but..." He shuddered. "It felt like someone was pushing me down, suffocating me with their invisible grip."

Charlie scooped up her candle and made to barrel past Darren, but his solid form prevented her from rushing down the hall. "Get out of my way!" She screamed so loud her voice cracked. "She needs me!"

Alex gathered the camera from the floor, supporting the device as if it were an infant. He felt awkward and useless once again. Everything was falling apart; his friends were getting hurt and worse... and he was the ringleader for this bloody circus; a showman with no direction and no sense of how to continue.

"Wait, Charlie..." Darren took a deep breath. Usually so composed, he fidgeted in this moment of uncertainty.

"Madicyn... she..." He flailed his arm, uselessly gesturing to the stairs. His candle wavered in his haste, and he quickly pulled his arm back as if his body would shield any force trying to extinguish it.

Alex felt the blood drain from his face. He gripped Charlie's shoulder. "I'm not leaving you; we'll find Sydney." He paused, studying Darren's lost features. "Stay here Darren, and collect yourself. We'll get Nikki and Whitney back upstairs, and we'll ride out the last hour together."

Darren nodded, "Yeah... together..." he whispered. He sunk on the bed and continued to stare at the candle's ever-diminishing wick.

Chapter Forty-Two

2:35 a.m. Handheld Camera

"Just wait a minute," Alex pleaded, gripping Charlie's arm as she marched down the hallway. "We don't know where we're going or what we're walking in to."

Charlie spun around so quickly, her candle's flame whipping dangerously close; Alex thought his sparse facial hair would be caught aflame. Charlie swung her arms wildly around the pitch-black expanse. "We didn't know what any of this was! We didn't know we'd be searching to see if any more of our friends were dead." Charlie's pupils were dilated to an impossible width, the left corner of her mouth stuck in an endless twitch. "I abandoned her, Alex! I promised her she wouldn't get hurt!"

Alex picked at the loose threads of his hoodie. What advice could he offer? "They're my friends too, Charlie. I'm just as scared as you. Don't act like you're the only one who lost someone." He turned from her to open the bathroom door.

"You're sick," Charlie seethed. She stepped uncomfortably close to Alex, grabbing his thin arm to twist him to face her again. Her frame was shaking with suppressed emotions. "You know all the right words, don't you? Just what you're supposed to say... but you're enjoying this, aren't you?"

"What?" Alex edged backward, away from Charlie's accusatory glare and the now blinding ray of light from her candle's flame. "Are you crazy, Charlie? Of course not! I just want to survive... just like you! You think I want to see my friends murdered?"

"Then why are you still filming, Alex? Why haven't you let go of the damn camera yet?"

The remaining air left Alex's lungs in a strong whoosh. The air between them stilled, the unsaid words thrumming an electric beat between them. Alex's own hand began to shake as it desperately clung to the camera; he still had trained on his best friend.

"Is this what you wanted, Alex? Your shot at fame?" Charlie's voice cracked.

Alex felt his mouth dry. A million denials crossed his mind but died before escaping his lips. He wanted to dismiss the accusations, but a small part of him whispered doubts. It was true, the idea of turning off the camera hadn't even occurred to him once.

"Turn it off, Alex," Charlie whispered. Alex didn't react. "I'm serious, Alex... turn it off now." With a scream, she lunged for him. He batted at her hand, but she kept advancing, screaming insults and accusations while clawing at his arm.

"Watch your candle Charlie!" Alex shouted over her. "Are you trying to burn me?"

"This is all your fault!" Charlie sobbed, shoving him firmly in the ribs, sending his thin frame reeling backward, his arms flailing and his candle flickering wildly. He collided with the bathroom door, his head making a hollow thump upon impact.

For a moment, the two were silent, their heavy breaths filling the space between them. Finally, Charlie offered a mumbled apology for her outburst but didn't help Alex to his feet. Alex also offered a half-assed sorry as he righted himself, reaching behind him to shut the bathroom door. He paused when his fingers brushed something sticky on the doorframe.

"Charlie..." he croaked.

She turned and saw Alex had grown a ghastly pale, his eyes the size of saucers. Her eyes darted to his white-knuckled grip on the knob. "What's in there, Alex?"

He shook his head. "Don't..." his eyes squeezed shut, as if to erase the image he'd just taken in. "Don't look."

Charlie felt a cold trickle slither down her spine. "Open it," she whispered. Alex wouldn't meet her eye. "Open it, dammit!"

Alex stepped aside. "You don't want to look, trust me." He sighed heavily. "But I won't stop you... I'll give you a minute. I'm going to grab Whitney and Nikki. Get Darren, and we'll meet up in the living room together to figure out the last hour together."

Chapter Forty-Three

2:40 a.m. Bathroom Camera

"Sydney..." Charlie thought she had steeled herself for what was beyond the door. She knew it wouldn't be pretty, and she knew her beloved Sydney was on the other side. However, she wasn't prepared for the gruesome sight before her.

The once cheerful pink walls were smeared with blood. Handprints scattered across the tile floor depicted a struggle. *Why was there so much blood?* It seemed impossible, so much had come from her dainty girlfriend.

Charlie stumbled across the room, slipping on the bloody smears in her haste.

Her hand shook as it cautiously reached out for the shower curtain. The shadow cast from the flame's glow distorted her fingers to claws, giving a sinister veil to the shroud. Clenching her eyes shut, she ripped the curtain open. Slowly, Charlie peeked and instantly wished she hadn't.

Stomach churning, she dropped to her knees as the walls melted away. Charlie forgot to breathe, forgot where she was and what was at stake, all that existed was the meaty lump that was formerly her girlfriend left in the tub. Bloody stumps oozed where her arms and legs previously attached, her mouth a twisted scream of horror, the jaw just barely hanging onto the rest of the skull. Bile rose in Charlie's throat as her eyes zeroed in on Sydney's gaping chest, seemingly torn in half. *Where was her heart?* The cavity was absent of the essential organ, and Charlie held back the temptation to dig around to find it.

"I'm so sorry..." She whispered, running her fingers through the matted hair. Her fingers slowly slid over Sydney's eyelids, shutting them forever.

Chapter Forty-Four

2:40 a.m. Bedroom Camera

"I'm not afraid... I've followed all the damn rules," Darren muttered to himself as he watched the flame dance teasingly before him. Every flicker made him jump, the bag of salt in his pocket burning against his thigh. *Would that truly save him from the supposed demon stalking them?* He licked his parched lips as the thought flitted across his mind. *Was it really only a few hours ago that Nikki and I were making out? It felt like a lifetime ago.*

Darren examined his hand, twisting it in the flame's glare and memorizing each criss-crossing line across his palm. He rubbed the hand over his face, relief flooding him when he felt his smooth skin. A shudder raced down his spine as the feeling of panic he'd battled only moments before wormed back into his mind. He had been on the couch, trying to keep his heavy eyelids open and preventing himself from dozing off, he'd heard Sydney screaming in the kitchen and felt frozen in place in the living room, as if a phantom force had held him down and disabled him from assisting her. Then, he felt as if a bucket of ice water had doused him, and he saw Sydney sobbing as she darted past him upstairs, slamming the bathroom door when she got up there. Darren intended to go after her, to see what the hell had freaked her out enough to break the rule that was supposed to save her. But his reflection in the foyer mirror distracted him enough to pause his rescue mission.

Darren couldn't comprehend that the terrified face gaping back at him was his own reflection. His perfectly tanned skin was peeling off his face, reveal sinewy muscle beneath. Raising a hand in disbelief, he only succeeded in pulling off another chunk of flesh, chalky bone peeking out underneath. Horrified, Darren watched as a handful of his thick hair slipped from his head in a ragged clump. Desperately, he tried to run his hand through the remaining locks and managed only to break off a finger, thick blood oozing from the gaping wound. His chest felt constricted, and Darren gaped for air as his body began to decay in front of him. It was the muffled scream from upstairs that broke his reverie, and with another glance at the mirror, it showed his face back to its handsome self.

"Shit!" He caught a movement in the corner of his eye, twitching, he brandished his diminishing candle as a weapon. It was just his reflection in the vanity mirror; his normal, healthy reflection. He forced a chuckle at his own expense as he felt as if he was starting to nod off again. Lazily, he paced over to the dresser, tilting the light to reflect on the various frames crowding the surface. Sydney and Charlie embracing at graduation, a few of the drama club members in exaggerated poses after the senior musical, and a group photo from a few years' past, Nikki's face ripped out and an emoji sticker winking in its place.

Nikki... Darren felt a pang of guilt. He could feel the shadow of her hand squeezing his, seeking his guidance, could see her icy eyes begging him not to leave her. And here he was, jumping at his own reflection, alone. He had to go back downstairs, find Nikki, and protect her...

Like you protected Madicyn? The snide voice reverberated in his head. *No! I didn't owe Madicyn anything.* She made it quite clear during their last breakup that she was independent and didn't want his help for anything. Darren wanted to remember Madicyn before the drama with Nikki, when her face was flushed with excitement, her eyes sparkling with more than just malice. Instead, it was replaced with the bloated corpse he found bent over the sink. Her once cruel mouth only a slab of meat now... her beautiful face sliced to ribbons...

Darren shook his head to free his thoughts. *I couldn't save Madicyn, but there was still a chance with Nikki. I am Darren Holt, dammit!* While his charm and good looks couldn't see him out of this particular situation, he knew he had to keep calm in order to survive.

An ear-piercing shriek ripped through the silence. It was coming from... outside?

"Help me, please!" The feminine voice was definitely outside. "Darren! Help!"

"Nikki?" Darren rushed to the window; the rain was still a hard drizzle, and he couldn't make out much in the murky grey. He squinted, trying to make sense of the dark shapes of the woods behind the house, trying to pinpoint the sporadic shrieks and screams that continued to echo around him.

"Darren! He... he's coming for me!"

There! He could see the flash of blonde in the dark. Nikki was slipping on the muddy terrain, heading for the line of trees just meters from the house. The window was freckled with raindrops, making her outline blurry and her features hard to distinguish. But her screams of terror were enough for Darren to act on. Setting his candle a safe distance from the sill, he tried prying open the window. It was stuck.

"Nikki!" Darren pounded on the glass, but her figure grew fainter the more she stumbled away, continuing to scream for help. "I'm coming, Nikki!" He heaved harder after fumbling with the lock mechanisms. With a hefty tug, the window gave way, sliding upward with sudden ease. Wasting no more time, Darren quickly popped the screen out of place. "I'm coming, Nikki!" He called out again, eyeing the drop to the attached garage's roof below him. An easy drop. He had to save her, and this was the quickest way to get to her.

Darren began to lean out, stretching his arm out as if to pluck her from the trees and back to safety, his sight focusing on where Nikki's silhouette had vanished. He braced himself against the frame, one leg stretched and ready to jump to save her until he felt the acidic burning on his outstretched arm. The rain had slowed to a consistent drizzle, but each drop caused Darren's skin to sizzle and fry.

Darren felt frozen, as if his body was glued to the window frame, completely stuck and helpless to watch the rain erode his skin. The olive tone he'd taken pride in was melting away to expose sinewy muscle beneath. A gust of wind burst forth, and with bulging eyes, Darren watched the muscle crumble as if made of dust, revealing bright white bone. His hand now completely void of any flesh; the skin on his arm also began melting from his body, creeping up to his neck and finally his face. Within minutes, all that remained was a grinning skeleton slumped over the windowsill, clothes barely staying draped over the thin bones.

Chapter Forty-Five

2:45 a.m.   Handheld Camera

"Charlie is right..." Alex sighed. He had flipped the screen, the lens pointing at his own forlorn face. With the night vision mode activated, his eyes glowed a sinister white. "I am sick... but I can't turn this camera off. I have to see how this ends." He was seated in the living room, waiting for his friends to come to him. His stomach was churning over the bloody massacre he'd seen in the bathroom. He still hadn't peeked in the kitchen where he knew Madicyn's body lay. Not to mention James' still covered corpse not too far from her.

Alex winced on the screen, realizing he was having his *Blair Witch* moment, but continued to mumble to the camera. As if it would ease his troubled thoughts and alleviate the guilt gnawing at him. "Sure, I read the rules... knew the risks... and yeah... maybe a part of me wanted this to be real." He stared at his own distorted image. "But I never wanted anyone to die. The thrill was in capturing something paranormal, maybe seeing someone's candle go out unexpectedly... but no one was supposed to die." His flame flickered dangerously wild, casting shadows upon his features. "Maybe I'm the real demon here..." he mused as his likeness shifted to something less recognizable.

BANG!

The door slamming was so loud, Alex swore he felt his bones reverberating. Charlie must have finished her goodbye to Sydney then. He listened to her scurry back down the hall to the bedroom. *Guess it's time to call Nikki and Whitney back upstairs.*

Shuffling to the basement door, careful not to glance at Madicyn's still frame frozen at the counter behind him, he trained his camera to once more focus on the gaping maw of black below.

"Whit? Nikki?" He called. "It's time for you to come upstairs!" Silence. Alex felt as if a finger traced from the base of his neck down his spine, a chill weaving down its wake. "No, no, no..." he whispered. With a deep gulp, he stepped on the first ledge. "Nikki? Are you hurt?" Nothing. "Whitney, what happened?"

The second stair creaked under his weight. Alex paused again, hoping for a glimpse of movement and straining to hear even the slightest noise. He descended the next steps quicker, continuing to call out.

"Al-ex!" Came the sing-song from the gaping darkness below the stairs.

He stilled, his blood frosting at the distorted lilt.

"Aren't you going to come down here and play?" There was a girlish titter, marred by something sinister in the undertone. "After all, isn't that why you wanted us all here tonight? The perfect cast of dolls for you to play with. Come on, Alex... direct us!" This time the laugh was closer to a high-pitched shriek.

Alex saw the glint of light just in time to dodge out of Whitney's way as she seemed to float out of the abyss toward him. The stairway was narrow, and the two barely squeezed together in the compact space. In the light of his candle, he saw Whitney's once beautiful face battered and scratched, her hand caked in blood and gripping a shattered shard of a mirror.

She pouted her split lip in a duckface. "What do you think, Mr. Director?" She batted her eyelashes, the pupils having completely overtaken the irises. "Am I ready for my close-up?" She lunged again, and he just barely ducked her swing. "Oh! I see we've reached the action sequence! Delightful!" she squealed.

Her next attack left Alex with no choice but to drop his beloved camera. After nudging his candle onto a step above him, he gripped her wrist; it became a surprisingly even battle as they wrestled, the jagged edge hovering dangerously close to his face.

"Come on, Alex!" Whitney cooed. "Don't you want to see your reflection? Your true reflection?"

Alex didn't want to see what she was toying with him about, but he couldn't resist slipping his gaze to the mirror that was precariously hovering over him. Gazing back wasn't his youthful skin or hazel eyes. Instead, a demonic face was reflected back. The eye was a brilliant yellow with a black slit of a pupil housed in blood red, scaly skin. Alex choked on his screams of horror.

Whitney giggled. "Don't you see, Alex? It's your true reflection! Now you're as dead on the outside as you are on the inside! Poetry!" With renewed strength, she began to drive the edge down, nicking his cheek. "Really, Alex. You need to learn to live a little!"

Alex could feel his muscles giving out beneath Whitney's constant weight. His knees began to buckle under him, and his balance faltered on the narrow steps. *James, Madicyn, Nikki, Whitney... I've failed them all.* Tears pricked his eyes with the realization. *They were dead because of me. And now I'm was going to join them in the afterlife, all because I wanted to make a stupid video.*

His legs gave out, and his hip landed hard on the step underneath him. Whitney tumbled down with him, the razor-sharp edge cutting deeper into his face. As he caught himself, his fingers brushed the abandoned camera... his lifeline once again.

"Whitney!" She glanced up at him again. "I'm ready for your close-up." With that, he flipped on the flash, the white light exploded in the darkness. Whitney hissed, covering her eyes from the glare. Alex took the moment of confusion to relinquish her grip on the shank, and he drove it into her shoulder before she could catch her bearings. With only a second of regret, Alex shoved Whitney; with a strangled cry, she fell backward, tumbling down to the bottom of the steps with a definitive thud followed by a loud crash.

Alex grabbed his candle and rushed down the remaining steps, scanning the empty basement to see a sticky pool of blood, Nikki lying face down, shards of glass dug deep into her back, her arm stretched out in a desperate attempt to flee in her last moments. One sticky rivulet trailed to the corner of the basement. Alex panned the camera up to show that one of the metal shelving units fell over, the heavy boxes piled on top with their contents strewn about, Whitney's leg poked out of the wreckage. Alex frantically dug through the mess of holiday decor, muttering desperate utterances, but upon clearing some of the junk it became obvious, Whitney hadn't survived the fall. Blood was seeping from a gash on her head and her ribs crushed from the heavy burden of the shelves.

Alex let himself sob as he took in the sight of two more dead friends.

Chapter Forty-Six

2:47 a.m. Bedroom Camera

"I... I can't..." Charlie sobbed. She dropped to her knees, slamming her fist on the ground. "Why?" Furiously, she wiped the tears off her cheeks.

There was no end to the horror, there was no winning the game. Sydney was quartered, and her heart was missing; for what? Charlie tried to recall the forums she and Alex had read, laughing at the accounts of terror and guessing how long the bloggers had thought through their stories before posting. But no, it wasn't some internet prank... they were warnings. Charlie and Alex had been too arrogant to heed those tales.

Charlie shivered as a cold breeze wrapped around her frame.

Wait... a breeze?

Complete numbness washed over Charlie. Her hand covered her mouth as once more, her stomach heaved at the grotesque picture before her. Darren's body lay limp in the window frame, his upper torso was corroded away completely, and she stared in horror at the bare bones remaining. She pulled him back through the window, not feeling comfortable leaving what was left of her friend dangling outside.

"Why, Darren?" She whispered. "You knew the rules!" Again, she slammed her fist against the floor. "Don't leave the house! That was the easiest rule to follow! This wasn't my fault!"

Charlie glanced around the room, taking in the pictures of Sydney's smiling face from nearly every surface. That girl loved to take pictures. Charlie smiled as old memories stirred of simpler times when the group was cohesive. That was before the hookups... and the subsequent breakups... and then the hooking up again. All the good memories shined brighter than any of the bad ones, the silly tiffs that drove the group nearly in half seemed but a blur.

"Aw, Babe," cooed a voice in Charlie's ear. "Why so sad? You know it hurts me to see you like that…"

Charlie whipped around. "Sydney…?"

Sydney's giggle was fainter, seeming to drift from the closet in the opposite corner. Charlie picked her way across the room, pausing in front of the white doors. *This had to be a trick, the Midnight Man didn't like to lose*, Charlie thought. *I had been so careful to follow the rules. Could he do this? Was it possible this demon would play dirty just to get me to slip up?*

Charlie whipped open the door. Using her candle to scan the depths of the closet, Charlie saw only her own hoodies and jackets she'd yet to pack, mashed with Sydney's blouses. With a heavy sigh, Charlie gripped the nearest blouse and ripped it from the hanger. She pressed her face into the soft material, inhaling the unique blend of lavender that seemed to follow Sydney wherever she went. Tears pricked her eyes, and she buried herself further into the shirt, breathing in the scent of the one she'd loved for so long, it was almost as if Sydney's arms were wrapped around her once again. Feeling Sydney's thin arms gripping her waist tightly, face pressed against her neck; she could almost hear her breathy giggle. Charlie let the fantasy take her, Alex's mocking cooing at their affection, Madicyn's sarcastic "so cute," followed by James faking a gag... even Nikki's cheer of "you go girl" and Darren's saucy wink. In her mind, she held Sydney tighter, feeling her girlfriend's grip tighten almost uncomfortably around her ribs.

"They're all gone now..." she whispered to herself.

One single tear rolled down Charlie's cheek as she lifted her candle to her face. Keeping her gaze trained on the photo of Sydney, she took only weeks ago; Charlie blew out her candle.

Chapter Forty-Seven

3:00 a.m.   Handheld Camera

"Charlie! Darren!" Alex screamed, slamming the basement door shut behind him. He stumbled blindly through the kitchen, his legs feeling the consistency of jelly. He could feel the warm blood still trickling down his face, but he didn't bother to wipe it away. He was more concerned about the blood soaking his fingerless gloves at the moment. Whitney's blood.

No, he reminded himself. *That creature was no longer Whitney. Would this nightmare ever end?* His hands shook so violently he feared he'd put out his candle. *What happens when the game is over?* Call the police? Convince them that a demon killed everyone? He clutched his camera tighter. "Proof." He whispered.

Alex hauled himself up the stairs, wasting no time rushing into the bedroom to share the horror of his encounter with Charlie and Darren. He stopped short when he heard only silence

"No, please!"

The stark white of the grinning skull immediately drew his attention. As if in a trance, Alex approached, he had to get a closer look to try and figure out what the hell happened. His trek was cut short as he tripped over something in the middle of the floor.

"What happened, Charlie?" He muttered, shrinking back to the threshold. As much as he didn't want to know, he couldn't look away. His gaze was forced to examine the cold corpse of a friend he used to consider a sister. The lighting was dim, but something was wrong with her torso; Alex cautiously ran a hand over her shirt, shifting the body to examine what was wrong. The sick crinkle proved Charlie's ribs had been broken, crushed inward, and potentially puncturing a lung. Perhaps a trick of his dying light… but Alex swore her mouth was… smiling?

Beyond Charlie was…

Alex vomited; it was all too much to process at once. His body was coated in a cold sweat, and he heaved until his stomach was empty, but it didn't stop. When the world finally stopped tilting, he staggered to his feet. Scooping up his candle, he rushed back down the stairs, running away from the terror and destruction.

"Help me!"

Alex skid to a halt at the bottom of the steps. "Charlie?" He yelled back up.

"Alex, help!" That time it sounded like Sydney.

His name became a chant, a blend of the familiar voices of his friend and a dark, unknown voice seeming to lay underneath it all.

"Leave me alone!" Alex screamed, swinging around to inspect the surrounding shadows.

Above the pounding of his heart and gasps for breath, Alex heard his name being whispered, continuing to mimic the voices of his now dead friends. "Alex, help!" From the basement staircase. "Please! Please!" the voice pleaded from the basement. The screams of anguish and terror echoed all around him.

Alex crumpled to the floor, hugging his knees and clawing at his ears, all while screaming for the assault to stop. The agony continued for what felt like eons. *Is this my torture? Am I to go mad, forever to hear the dying shrieks of my friends?* He watched as the weak flame on his candle flickered and danced as it burned away the wick. For a moment, Alex actually wished for it to go out, for the Midnight Man to just end the horror.

As if reading his thoughts, the flamed winked out.

Alex sat up as the voices were swept away on a sudden, chilly gust. He clutched his handheld camera, which he had carelessly discarded in his panic, noting the bright glow from the screen. *Is this the cause of the terror?* Alex paused as he thought of the strict rules against any source of light... had he doomed them from the start? Shaking himself from his melancholy reverie, Alex utilized the zoom, he explored the thick darkness that seemed to be closing in on him.

A flash of lime green gave him pause. With his heart thudding madly against his ribs, he focused the lens on three glowing numbers. 3:33.

"No way…" Alex whispered. He strained to hear past his own rapid breath and heartbeat but was only met with a static silence. The storm had passed… the power was back on! The Game was over. He'd managed to survive. Tears stung Alex's eyes as the implications of it all hit him.

Turning the camera on himself, he whispered, "I win… I'm sorry." Gently, he placed the camera on the end table and slowly made his way to the front door. He paused only a moment, hesitating to believe he'd actually escape. With a deep breath, he twisted the knob and stepped out onto the porch.

Soon, Alex's figure disappeared from the view of the camera. Slowly, the door began to creak. A sinister chuckle echoed through the empty house. A low voice rumbled, "Game over."

The door clicked shut.

Epilogue

Hello Minions! Your favorite high priestess here with a quick update. As you know, this blog is always your number one source for all things paranormal and Pagan! Well, do we have a scoop today!

Remember last month, when that insane story dropped about the "murder house"? You know, the one with the six dead bodies, completely mutilated? Rumor had it that there was some insane evidence that left the police department scratching their heads. Well, loyal followers, it appears there was a leak!

Linked below, you'll find the video of what was found that day in the house. That's right, everything was recorded in full!   We've got the exclusive!

Let me tell you, it's pretty crazy! Apparently, the victims were playing the *Midnight Game*; some ritual involving summoning a demon, and they paid for it.

So, click the link below, check out the video, and tell me what you think. Demonic rampage or just a well-edited video?   Is the *Midnight Man* real or is it some crazy hoax? Guess there's only one way to find out. That's right; check back here next week after I play the *Midnight Game* to see the results!

-Your Pagan Priestess

Author's Note

Hello, readers!

The Midnight Game is a real game, though it is not advised that you play at home! In researching for this book, I used a few sites to get information on the rules and to see how the urban legend has developed over the years. The game was originally posted on Creepy Pasta and has grown in popularity over the years, adding different variances the longer it's existed. For more information about the game and its origins, you can visit the following websites:

https://creepypasta.fandom.com/wiki/Midnight_Game

https://www.unexplained-mysteries.com/forum/topic/209190-the-midnight-game/

https://www.reddit.com/r/Paranormal/comments/7efnc7/the_origins_of_the_midnightman/

Chelsea Gouin

A Michigan native, Chelsea Gouin lives on the East Side of Detroit as a Special Education Teacher. Writing has been a lifelong passion, especially when it causes a thrill. When not writing or educating, she's found hunting for spirits and investigating local legends.